HENNING MANKELL is one of Sweden's best-selling authors. He has published a number of plays and novels for adults, many of them drawing on his experience in Africa. For children and young adults he writes poetic, intimate stories with strong narrative appeal, and these have won him several awards, including the prestigious Astrid Lindgren Prize.

Playing with Fire is the second novel about Sofia, the heroine of *Secrets in the Fire*. She is a real person, a friend of Henning Mankell, and her moving story has been adapted for film.

ANNA PATERSON is an award-winning translator who has translated many literary projects from Scandinavian languages and German into English and Swedish. In 2000, she won the Bernard Shaw Prize for Literary Translation for her translation of *Forest of Hours* by Kerstin Ekman. In her English translation of Henning Mankell's *Playing with Fire*, she has been true to the original style of writing and the author's clear, sensitive approach to the realities of life in Mozambique. Anna lives in Scotland.

playing
with fire

❧

HENNING MANKELL

translated by Anna Paterson

ALLEN&UNWIN

This edition published in 2002

Copyright © Henning Mankell, 2001

First published by Rabén & Sjögren Bokförlag, Sweden, 2001 as *Eidens Gåta*
Copyright English translation © Anna Paterson 2001

Allen & Unwin
83 Alexander Street
Crows Nest NSW 2065
Australia
Phone: (61 2) 8425 0100
Fax: (61 2) 9906 2218
Email: info@allenandunwin.com
Web: www.allenandunwin.com

National Library of Australia
Cataloguing-in-Publication entry:

Mankell, Henning, 1948- .
Playing with fire.

ISBN 978 1 86508 714 6

1. Poor girls—Mozambique—Fiction. I. Paterson, Anna. II. Title.

839.7

Cover photograph Nick Ray/Lonely Planet Images
Cover image by Steve Hunt, Pigs Might Fly Productions
Cover and text design by Jo Hunt
Typeset by Midland Typesetters
Printed by McPherson's Printing Group

3 5 7 9 10 8 6 4

In memory of Rosa

I want to tell you one more story.
This one is about Sofia
and her sister Rosa.

It's not quite dawn in Africa
and Sofia is barely awake.
It's still dark
but the sun will soon rise over the horizon
like a red fireball

to light one more day in Sofia's life . . .

TRANSLATOR'S NOTE

Mozambique was once ruled from Portugal and people still speak Portuguese. They also use local languages. Some of the words used in this book are explained here.

machamba	field
A *Mupfana wa N'wheti*	Moonboy (in a local language called Ronga)
Meticais	Meticais is the Mozambique currency. It is abbreviated to MZM. One MZM is spoken of as 'one metical'. In January 2001, the value was approximately 17,331 meticais to one US dollar.
curandiero	magician, 'witchdoctor'
capulana	colourful lengths of cloth that women wrap around themselves as skirts or dresses
saia	skirt
A *Gorda*	The fat one (woman)
O *Chapeu*	The hat

The Dollar/MZM exchange rate comes from the *CIA World Factbook*, which has a good map and numerous interesting facts about Mozambique.

The web address is: www.cia.gov/cia/publications/factbook/

ONE

Sofia woke one morning feeling that something strange was about to happen, something she had never known about before. Maybe it would turn out to be one of the most important events in her life.

As usual she had woken up just before Mrs Mukulela's rooster started crowing. That rooster was such a nuisance, she thought. No one in the village liked it. It always started crowing far too early, long before the first pale ribbons of morning light began to show above the mountains to the east of the village. Mr Temba used to tell Mrs Mukulela off because she wouldn't get rid of her rooster, which obviously had no idea that there was a proper time to crow. Mr Temba lived in the hut opposite Mrs Mukulela's place. He had threatened to kill that rooster many times. Once, when he was back from Boane market after an especially good day selling the baskets he made, he had offered to buy the rooster. He wanted to kill it and eat it for supper, he said. Mrs Mukulela had patted her big breasts into place under the cloth she wore wrapped around her body, and replied tartly that her rooster was not for sale. She had sounded quite fierce.

Lying there in the dark, Sofia giggled quietly at the memory. She liked them both and felt sure that Mr Temba and Mrs Mukulela weren't actually quarrelling about the rooster. Mr Temba was cross because Mrs Mukulela refused to move in with him. They both lived alone. Mrs Mukulela's husband had gone away to work in the South African mines and found himself another woman to live with. Mr Temba was a widower. His wife had died several years ago.

They kept having these quarrels because they cared for each other, Sofia thought.

Then she giggled some more, this time at Mrs Mukulela's breasts. They were very large, and every time she got upset she'd start pushing at them, as if they were in the way of her bad temper.

Rosa was sleeping on the floor next to her bed.

Sofia could hear her breathing in the darkness. In the other room, separated from theirs by a piece of cloth hanging across the doorway, their mother and two younger brothers were sleeping. The sleepy noises they made felt good and safe to hear. Sofia liked this time in the morning when she was the only one awake.

She stayed where she was and thought about the day

ahead. First thing, she'd put on the two plastic legs she'd had to wear since the day she stepped on a landmine. Her sister Maria had died that day. Every morning, while she strapped on her legs, she'd be chatting with Maria. It was a fact that Maria had been dead for four years by now, but still Sofia knew that her sister was coming to see her in the mornings somehow.

Strangely enough, Maria appeared not to have grown at all. The Maria in Sofia's mind looked exactly like the Maria from that dreadful morning. She must be coming to visit from the other world under the ground, which dead people travelled to. The dead were buried in the earth and in the blackness deep down there a door would open into their own world. Or maybe it was more like following a river that started as a trickle and grew wider. Then a boat would come along, its sail filling with the underground wind, the buried person would step on board and the boat would drift along to reach the world of the dead. In her thoughts Sofia often asked Maria what that other world was like and heard her sister answer, saying that it was just like the village where Sofia lived. Everything was the same, just ordinary. Truly, there was no difference between being dead and being alive.

Maria would vanish after their chat. She wore a white dress, and seemed to slip into the beams of sunlight, as if becoming part of them.

Every morning began the same way. Sofia's legs were leaning against the wall, waiting for her. Then Maria appeared. Afterwards Sofia went out in the yard to wash. To get to the well where she collected the washing water, she had to walk along the road towards the town. She had learnt to balance the bucket of water on her head, even though she still needed two crutches to get about. When she had washed and checked her face in the broken piece of mirror that she'd once found on the way to school, it was time to start helping her mother, Lydia. She would already be about, starting up the fire to prepare breakfast before she set out walking to the *machamba* where she grew vegetables and corn. Sofia's job was to sweep the yard. Once that was done, Rosa would have left to start her work on the plot of land next to their hut. It was just a small field between Mrs Mukulela's house and the road to the marketplace. That afternoon, Sofia was to mend a pair of trousers for Mr Temba and carry on with cutting out a dress-pattern for Rosa.

This morning would mostly be just as usual, though.

Perhaps the only unusual thing was that she wasn't going to school. The teacher, Miss Adelina, had told everyone that the leaking school roof was going to be repaired. At last, the money had come from somewhere, and the pupils had to stay at home for a day or two this week.

Sofia thought that getting one extra day off school would be nice. No more than that, because she liked school. In

10

a remote corner of her mind was an image of herself wearing a white coat—she was Doctor Sofia. She had told no one, not even Rosa, of this dream of hers. Sometimes it almost frightened her, because it was so awesome and anyway, so far away in time. But it came back to her every day. It was like a beautiful, stubborn butterfly fluttering about inside her head and refusing to leave.

Soon it would be light.

The rooster would start crowing first. She pulled her blanket up to her chin and wondered what special thing might happen today.

Would she fall in love? Maybe a boy would come walking along the road, someone who wouldn't mind her false legs? Thinking about it made her feel hot all over. She tried to visualise what he might look like.

At just that moment the rooster crowed.

Rosa turned but didn't wake. Sofia, who loved Rosa, reached out her hand to pat her sister's plaited hair. Rosa was seventeen, three years older than Sofia, and different from the two little boys, because Sofia could talk to her about everything. They often laughed together.

The morning had begun. She went on stroking Rosa's hair.

She had no idea of the dreadfulness that the new day would bring.

TWO

Now and then Sofia would think about the way life was made up mostly of events that nobody could predict. Even if you planned what to do, something unexpected always seemed to happen. Sofia remembered clearly the first time she started to think about this. It was after the great disaster, which had happened on the morning of what should have been a perfectly ordinary day. Sofia had stepped on a buried landmine. Her sister Maria had died in the explosion, and Sofia had lost both her legs. That was when she learnt that nothing was certain and knowable in advance. This was true for everything in life. At bedtime, you couldn't predict if it would rain or not when you woke up the next morning. There was no telling when your stomach would feel sore or when an itching mosquito bite would turn up in the kind of spot on your body that someone else would have to rub for you.

Normally, there was no telling if the day ahead would be good or bad. All you could do was hope for the best.

Sofia had tried to speak to Rosa about these thoughts more than once.

But Rosa wasn't interested. She thought Sofia was being childish. Besides, Rosa was almost always in love nowadays, and all she had time for then was the new boy.

The sisters felt especially close when Sofia plaited Rosa's hair. It was a good time for telling each other some of their secret thoughts—but not all. Sofia knew that Rosa kept some things to herself, just as she did. Maybe people never got so close that they could speak openly about all their feelings and dreams. You have a cave in your mind, where special thoughts are kept and nobody else is ever shown the way in.

But Rosa and Sofia seemed to share everything that mattered. Rosa was the older and because she had lived for longer, she had experienced more. She had stories to tell about things that were unknown to Sofia. The most important was called Love. Sofia listened carefully. She stored away what Rosa said in her memory.

There was another matter that formed an invisible barrier between them.

Rosa had never stepped on a landmine. She still walked on the legs she had been given at birth. Every morning, Sofia had to strap on two plastic rods with a shoe stuck on at one end, and remove them again each night.

There were times when Sofia reminded herself that she was not alone in having lost Maria. Maria had been Rosa's sister, too, of course. But somehow Rosa seemed not to mourn Maria in the same way as Sofia did. Maria never visited Rosa in the mornings. Or, at least, Rosa had never said anything about any visits. Surely she would have done. Sofia always thought before she spoke, but Rosa was different. She found it hard not to start talking eagerly the moment she felt there was an exciting story to tell.

Some thoughts and feelings were hard to speak about.

Sofia was often envious of Rosa's real legs. Rosa walked beautifully, easily, with swinging hips. Sofia could never learn to walk like that and she would always need to support herself on at least one crutch. Her gait was stiff, as if she were walking on knee-high stilts, and that's how it would always be. It was really difficult to admit that she felt envious. It wasn't Rosa's fault that just Sofia and Maria had been out playing together on the landmine morning. Sofia knew that she should be ashamed of envying Rosa. But some mornings, while she was waiting for the rooster to crow, her thoughts would make her so angry that she wanted to hit Rosa as she slept.

Besides, Rosa was more beautiful than she was.

With or without her legs, Sofia didn't have as beautiful a body and as lovely a face as Rosa. Sofia was heavily built, and Rosa was tall and slim. Already, Sofia had bigger breasts than Rosa did and Rosa's breasts were just the right size.

Sometimes at night they examined their naked bodies thoroughly, in spite of giggling all the time. They would pat and prod each other in the light of a candle. If the noise disturbed Lydia, she'd call out from the other room and ask what they were up to. Then they would stop at once. But when Lydia was snoring again, they'd start whispering once more in the dark. There was always so much to talk about and most interesting of all were the boys, who were trying hard to get to go out with Rosa.

Sofia got up, strapped on her legs, dressed and went outside. Lydia was already up and busy lighting the fire.

Sofia washed her face. Rosa stepped outside, yawned and stretched. One of her many boyfriends had given her a cream that she had rubbed into her face. Her skin gleamed when she lifted her head towards the sun. Sofia immediately felt another pang of envy. Sofia's skin would never be as smooth and glowing as Rosa's. Maybe she'd never meet a boy who cared to give her a cream like the one Rosa had.

Rosa walked up to Sofia.

'I can't understand why I'm so tired,' she said.

'It's because you don't get enough sleep,' Lydia told her sternly. 'You stay out far too late at night. And there are far too many boys running after you.'

Lydia kept stirring the boiling water in the iron pot, but Sofia noticed the quick glance she shot in the direction of Rosa's belly. She had been doing that every morning for quite a while. Sofia wondered what Lydia was looking for. Was she trying to find out if Rosa was going to have a baby, or what? It was hard to know what Lydia thought.

Rosa went to sit in the shade of the hut. Sofia came over and leaned against the wall next to her.

'I'm so tired,' Rosa said again. 'It doesn't make any difference how much I sleep. I feel exhausted all the time.'

'Are you ill then?'

Rosa shook her head.

'Nothing hurts anywhere.'

They didn't speak about that any more.

Breakfast was ready. The family gathered round the fire. Lydia served helpings of corn porridge for everyone. Sofia helped her second-youngest brother with his food. Alfredo, who was six, ate slowly so that the meal would last as long as possible. Faustino was not yet four.

Sofia was not sure who Faustino's father was. Sofia's father, who was also the father of Alfredo, Maria and Rosa, had been killed by bandits at the time of the last war. There was one faded picture of him, a tattered black-and-white photograph. Lydia had told them that a proper photographer had taken it when she and their dad had been newlyweds in South Africa. Dad had been working in a diamond mine. When Sofia felt down-hearted, she would pull out the photograph from its place between the pages of Lydia's hymnbook and look at it. In her thoughts she often asked Maria if she and Dad stayed together now that they were both dead. Maria never replied to that.

Sofia had tried to find out who Faustino's father was.

But his identity was one of Lydia's secrets, and she would not tell. Now and then Rosa and Sofia talked about it. Late one night, just before falling asleep, Rosa had whispered to Sofia that Mr Temba might be Faustino's father. Sofia was quite bewildered by this. Could Lydia really have felt so lonely that she had let Mr Temba sleep over in their hut? It was one thing that Sofia was fond of Mr Temba, and quite another to imagine that he might have been to bed with Lydia and fathered Faustino. Sofia refused to believe it. Rosa had become evasive and said she wasn't sure anyway.

Once, Sofia asked Lydia straight out.

She had chosen her moment carefully, because it was a difficult subject. Lydia had a hot temper, and could suddenly become furious. Sofia waited until Lydia was in a good mood and then asked her question, trying to sound casual, as if neither the question nor the answer mattered much one way or the other.

Lydia just laughed. 'A really nice man came along one day—and then he went on his way again,' she said.

Sofia had not asked any more questions. Lydia disliked being nagged by her children. Still, Sofia minded not knowing who her brother Faustino's father was.

Everything seemed perfectly ordinary.

Mrs Mukulela dropped in to say Good Morning. She was always curious about her neighbours and would look around to check if the yard was swept and tidy, or if any of the children wore something special, like a new T-shirt. They hardly ever did and this pleased Mrs Mukulela, who did not want anything about her neighbours to change—at least not change for the better. Mrs Mukulela liked being the person who wore the most beautifully patterned cloth as a body-wrap, and kept the happiest hens that laid the most eggs.

On her morning walk along the road she always stopped and quarrelled for a while with Mr Temba. He would have been up and about since dawn, when he settled in the shade of his hut to work on his baskets.

Lydia tied Faustino in place on her back, picked up her hoe and started walking to the *machamba*, a cultivated area in the foothills of the mountains. These fields were a couple of kilometres away from the village. The peaks of the mountains were barely visible in the heat haze. Lydia walked quickly, as if the day were too short for all the things she had to do.

Sofia watched her disappearing figure. Lydia looked thin and worn. She had given birth to nine children. Four were still alive. She had seen five of her children die and Maria was one of them. Sofia observed her mother hurrying along the road and wondered what she was thinking. She had borne children who had died, and every day she had to walk all the way to her field, as fast as she could, to tend the vegetables that were her only source of income. She never earned much from selling them.

Now Lydia had vanished into the sunlight, the way Maria did.

Sofia couldn't help wondering if she would become like Lydia one day—not quite the same, because she would never be such a fast walker. Sofia's crutches would always be with her. Besides, she wasn't sure if she would ever have any children of her own.

She kept looking along the road. For once, there was no one about.

Then she screwed up her eyes to peer at the place where Lydia had gone out of sight. No one came, no boy who might have stopped and looked at her without minding that she had no legs and was leaning on her crutches.

Sofia sighed and turned back to their yard.

Rosa had got up from her place by the wall and bent over to grab her hoe. Sofia frowned, because Rosa looked so awkward when she lifted the hoe. It looked as if it had doubled in weight since yesterday. Rosa swung the hoe onto her shoulder, straightened up and started to walk towards the small plot of ground near their hut. Next to it was Mrs Mukulela's place. Her hens were all outside, scratching around for food.

Sofia stayed where she was and watched Rosa.

At first there seemed to be nothing out of the ordinary. Then Sofia realised that Rosa's gait had changed. She usually stepped out lightly, with straight back and swinging hips. Now she seemed to be dragging herself along, walking as if every step hurt her. Sofia screwed up her eyes and kept watching. Rosa had reached their field now. She raised the hoe.

Then it fell out of her hand.

Rosa sank down on her knees.

Sofia caught her breath. She grabbed her crutches and hopped along to Rosa.

'What's the matter?' she asked.

'I don't know,' Rosa replied. 'I'm just feeling so tired.'

Sofia was looking at her and thinking of how thin Rosa had grown lately. These thoughts were painful and it felt as if something inside Sofia had hit her hard. Then her stomach went very cold. She felt frightened. It cannot be true, she said to herself. Not Rosa, not my sister.

Rosa was looking up at Sofia. Her face was glistening, but it was not the boyfriend's face-cream that made her face so shiny. It was sweat.

Sofia bent down over her sister. With a trembling hand, she reached out and touched Rosa's forehead. Rosa had a fever. She was ill.

Sofia felt as if a cold lump had formed in her stomach and was growing larger. The sun itself seemed to have gone down and night suddenly fallen.

THREE

Sofia helped Rosa back to the hut and made her lie down on the bed.

Rosa wanted to be on the floor, her usual sleeping place. Sofia would not let her. Rosa was ill and had to be in the bed. It was because of Sofia that they had a bed at all. She found it hard to get up from the floor without her legs. Mr Temba had given her the bed as a coming-home present when she returned from her long stay in hospital. Mr Temba had got it as part of a barter deal with a school teacher in Boane, who had acquired it in exchange for an old bicycle.

Rosa was settling down in the bed.

'Nothing hurts,' she said. 'I'm just so tired.'

'You're running a temperature,' Sofia said.

Rosa looked at her. 'Why does your voice sound so shaky?'

'It doesn't.'

Rosa kept looking at her. 'Listen, I'm not ill.'

'You do have a temperature. But I'm sure it's nothing serious.'

Then Rosa put her head back on the pillow and closed her eyes.

Sofia stayed and watched her. Rosa had been quite right. Sofia's voice had been shaking because she was so scared. The chill inside her was still there. All the time, she tried to convince herself that she was making a mistake. There was nothing really wrong with Rosa—she was just tired, maybe a little too hot. It could happen to anyone. In a few days she would be fine again.

But inside her a voice was saying something quite different.

The voice was arguing, pointing out that Rosa had dropped the hoe and sunk to the ground. Fever was not something that just happened for no reason. Then there was Rosa's thinness. That was the worst thing. The voice inside Sofia's head was shouting now. Why hadn't she reacted earlier? Why hadn't she taken any notice when Rosa started failing to finish her food? This was something completely new. During the last few months, Rosa had scraped large portions of rice or corn back into the big pan after practically every meal.

Rosa opened her eyes again.

'I've got a headache. The light's so bright.'

Sofia had been sitting on the edge of the bed. She picked up one of her crutches and prodded the curtain. It was made from old pieces of cloth that she had sewn together to fit the window.

'Would you like some water?' Sofia asked.

Rosa shook her head. 'I'll just sleep for a while,' she said. 'I'll be fine afterwards. You'd better go and keep an eye on Alfredo so he doesn't get up to something.'

Rosa was right, of course.

Alfredo must not be left alone. As Sofia got up from the bed and went outside, she thought of how she had happened to have this day off school, and what the meaning of that might be. Maybe life mostly consisted of lots of unpredictable events, but it was also true that sometimes things fell into place without any planning at all. Take today, for instance: the school had got the money to repair the roof, so she had to stay at home, and on that very day Rosa dropped the hoe.

Alfredo was sitting on the ground in front of the hut. He was drawing in the sand with a stick. For his age, he was a big boy, almost fat. He was wearing a pair of torn trousers, nothing else. The trousers had been Mr Temba's, but he had given them to Sofia in return for her mending some of his shirts. It was time to mend some more now, she thought.

Sofia could not make out what Alfredo was drawing in

the sand: it seemed to be a person.

'Who's that?' she asked.

'I don't know,' Alfredo replied.

'You mustn't get too close to the fire,' Sofia admonished him.

Alfredo only nodded. Sofia realised he thought that she was nagging. Even though he was only six, he knew well enough what he was not allowed to do. He almost always did as he was told.

Sofia went across to where Rosa's hoe was lying in their small field. She could hear Mrs Mukulela singing in the distance. She always sang loudly and kept hitting the wrong notes. Besides, her tunes never seemed to make sense, and the words were not set out in proper verses. Sofia listened.

My hens are just fine
but I need plenty more.
Maybe I should get myself a dog.
There's a broken nail on my left big toe . . .

Sofia shook her head. Honestly, Mrs Mukulela was not much good at making up songs.

She picked up the hoe from where it had fallen. It was no heavier than it had been yesterday.

Still, Rosa had dropped it today. Sofia carried it back

to the hut and propped it up against the wall. Lydia got upset if tools weren't properly looked after. The field needed weeding, but Rosa was too tired to do it. She had a fever and was lying down indoors. Sofia would do her work for her. Later.

First, Sofia needed to think. She sat down on one of the low wooden stools that were their only chairs, after pulling it into the shade of the hut. Sitting there, she could keep an eye on Alfredo.

She put her hand over her belly.

Inside, her stomach still felt quite cold. Sofia tried to think of something that was funny and had nothing to do with Rosa. It wasn't possible. Her thoughts kept going back to when she was in hospital. She had spent almost a year there after her accident.

In the hospital she had always been in general wards with many other people. When there were more ill people than beds, two patients had to share the same bed. At other times, patients were placed on straw mats under or between the beds—wherever there was room. Many were very ill, and each day there was at least one death.

For a long time a young man with bad burns occupied the bed next to Sofia's. He had been injured when his hut caught fire. He never spoke and no one ever came to visit him. One day, just before the afternoon meal, he died.

The next day there was a new patient in the bed. It

was a girl. She had been carried in on a stretcher and did nothing but sleep for the first few days. When she finally woke, she and Sofia started talking. They told each other their names and the names of their home villages. Then the new patient, who was called Deolinda, asked Sofia what was wrong with her. Sofia told the story of her accident and pulled back the sheet to show Deolinda the bandaged stumps that remained of her legs.

Now it was Sofia's turn to ask Deolinda why she had to be in hospital. The answer was unexpected. 'I'm dying,' Deolinda said. She was smiling.

Her smile somehow seemed to come from a great distance away. Sofia had never seen that kind of smile before. She learnt that people who knew they were close to death did not always weep or scream. The dying, too, could smile, even those—like Deolinda—who were only nineteen years old.

Mrs Mukulela had stopped singing. From the hut across the road a woman's voice was rising in anger. She was shouting accusations at her husband. Sofia picked up something about the man being lazy, but couldn't be bothered listening.

In her thoughts she returned to the hospital.

Deolinda had explained why she was dying. She had caught an illness Sofia had never heard of before. It was an infection with a virus that never left you, once it had found its way into the body. You could have it inside you and live for quite a long time, but sooner or later it would kill you.

Deolinda had also described how she caught the infection. Sofia remembered feeling hot with embarrassment at the time. No one had ever spoken to her so frankly about what surely had to be a great secret: the things that men and women do together in the dark. Deolinda had been very open. She had met this boy, whom she liked very much. They started going out, and slept with each other. After a year or so, he had become seriously ill. Things had moved rapidly from then on. He had stopped eating, a nasty rash spread all over his body, his hair fell out and he became so tired that finally he couldn't get out of bed. He died a few months later.

The doctor who had been looking after him had asked Deolinda to come to the hospital and give a blood sample. After a few days he contacted her again to let her know that she had the disease that had killed her boyfriend. He had told her what kind of illness it was. How one can be a carrier of it for many years without realising. How there was no way one could tell, by just looking, if someone was infected or not. The infection spread from person to person in different ways. Touching, hugging and so on were all right. But if people made love, the virus could pass from one to the other.

Sofia remembered everything Deolinda had told her.

'That's why I'm dying,' Deolinda had said. 'I loved him, you see. He didn't want to infect me. It's nobody's fault that I'm dying. I want to live. But I'll die anyway.'

Sofia was watching Alfredo. A dog came padding along the road. By now the sun was high in the sky. The heat was like fingertips pressing on her skin.

It can't be true, Sofia thought, and slapped her stomach to chase away the cold thing inside her. Rosa won't have the same illness as Deolinda. She'll get better soon, maybe after just a few days. I mustn't lose another sister. I'm imagining things. It's not serious. Rosa is asleep in the hut now. Lydia is right, though. Rosa had been running about far too much in the evenings.

Sofia felt a bit better. Her stomach seemed more normal.

She rose, took the hoe and walked to the small field. Alfredo was still drawing in the sand. Sofia knew that he was quite capable of dreaming on like that for hours.

She was just about to lift the hoe when she saw someone coming down the road. She shaded her eyes with her hand, trying to see who it was. The sunlight was very strong. It was a boy whom she could not recognise. She felt sure she had never even seen him before.

He stopped when he caught sight of Sofia, and smiled at her. She sensed rather than saw that he was looking straight at her, and started as if she had been struck.

Rosa's hoe hit the ground for the second time that day.

FOUR

Is it possible to know beforehand that something unforgettable is going to happen? Ever since that day, Sofia asked herself that question many times, but never felt sure of the answer. She had stood there among the weeds, holding the hoe, and just glanced down the road. A boy came walking along. That was all. She had been quite absorbed by her worries about Rosa, who was ill in bed with a fever.

But it had been a magic moment. Lydia had stories about moments like that—when wonderful, utterly unexpected things happened. For instance, there had been a time when Lydia had no food left at all. Sofia had been only little at the time. The last grains of corn meal and rice were finished and Lydia could no longer feed her children. The harvest had failed after a year of drought. The rain had fallen in a few desolate bursts, and most of the time it had not rained at all.

Lydia had told Sofia this story one evening when they

were sitting together by the fire. At the time she had been in terrible despair and decided to walk into town to beg. On the way, she had found quite a valuable note.

'Nobody would lose such a large sum of money,' she said. 'Someone put it there for me to find.'

Magic moments do exist.

Sofia knew that, and not only because Lydia had told her. Sofia had experienced them, too.

Her best magic moment had happened one morning when she first felt that Maria had come to be with her. Even if Maria existed only in her thoughts, it seemed extraordinary that Sofia could see her sister so clearly, speak to her, and hear her voice. And then watch as she vanished into the sunlight.

Afterwards it occurred to Sofia that the boy on the road had made her feel just the way she had imagined when she had woken up that morning. She'd had a sense that something miraculous would happen.

Thinking about it helped to convince her that Rosa did not have that dreadful disease after all. She was simply tired and her fever would be gone tomorrow. She would take the hoe, lift it almost over her head and swing it without losing her grip. When she was in the right mood, Rosa was a hard worker. Soon the weeds would be cleared from their plot of land.

The boy had stopped further along the road. Sofia hid one of her crutches behind her—one crutch was better than two. In her heart she knew that the boy had already noticed how difficult it was for her to move. Still, she felt it looked better if one crutch was out of the way. She glanced down at her legs. The length of cloth she had wound around her hips reached all the way down to her shoes. It was important that nothing of her plastic legs showed.

The boy was coming closer. Still, he didn't step over the low shrubs, which grew along the edge of their yard.

'Please, could you help me?' he said.

Sofia tried to remember all the things about talking to boys that Rosa had taught her. Like: if a boy speaks to you, it won't do to look interested. Answer, but not eagerly. Don't use too many words, only what's necessary.

'How do you mean?'

'I'm trying to find my uncle. His name is Lucas Macassa. I was told that he lives round here.'

Sofia tried to remember. No one called Macassa came to mind. She could have said No. Nothing else. But instead she said something different. It would be nice to keep the boy talking for a little longer. Especially now that she had spotted Mrs Mukulela standing in the shade of a banana tree, watching them. She must have noticed the boy and decided to keep an eye open.

'What does he do?' Sofia asked.

'He used to be a baker. Now, I'm not sure.'

'There's no bakery in our village.'

The boy considered this. Sofia pulled at her blouse. She had discovered some dirty marks and hoped they wouldn't show too much.

'I'm sure he must have settled down somewhere near here,' the boy said. 'Have I got it right? Is the village along the road called Mebena?'

'Why not?' Sofia felt rather pleased with her answer. Rosa had instructed her that it was good to answer a question from a boy with another question. It showed that you had a mind of your own.

'I don't know,' the boy said. 'But if it's Mebena, then my uncle lives here.'

Sofia didn't want him to go away. The trouble was, she couldn't think of many more things to say. She couldn't lie and tell him how to get to a hut that didn't exist.

Or could she?

Rosa had said nothing about this kind of thing. Then suddenly, without her realising how it had happened, Sofia's mind was made up.

'Maybe I know of someone called Macassa,' she said. 'If I'm right, then he lives at the far end of the village from here.'

She nodded towards the village. The huts were built in long rows down the slope of the hill.

'Please come back if you don't find him,' she went on.

The boy nodded and walked away.

Sofia was watching him. He was about Rosa's age, she thought. He was tall and slim and wore his hair cut short. Sofia wondered what running her hand over his head might feel like. She kept looking until he had disappeared down the slope. Then she went over to Alfredo, who was still engrossed in his drawings in the sand. Over and over he created figures, all looking different, and then rubbed them out. Sofia bent over him, closed her eyes and stroked his head. Alfredo, too, had his hair cut very short. Lydia wanted it that way to keep the head-lice away.

Sofia returned to the field where she had dropped the hoe. In one way, at least, it was useful that Rosa was lying ill in the hut. She shouldn't want to think this, but couldn't help herself. The reason was that if Rosa had been working outside, the boy would have looked only at her. He would not even have noticed Sofia. I'm the prettiest only when nobody else is around, she thought. Just for once, Rosa can surely let me be the one the boys want to talk to.

Once she realised what was going through her mind, she pushed it away immediately.

Rosa was ill. It was bad of Sofia to think about her in that way.

Sofia was working.

It was difficult to keep her balance while she hoed. She was soon soaked in sweat. Mrs Mukulela listened to her radio, which was powered by an old car battery. Once a week she put it in her wheelbarrow and pushed it all the way to the garage to charge it. The garage was near the river, and to get there and back took Mrs Mukulela a whole day. The radio was not very good, anyway. It made more scratchy noises than music.

The soil was dry. The hoe tore up earth, stones and dust.

Now and then Sofia straightened her back and looked down at the village. Would he come back? She wasn't sure, but knew that she hoped he would.

Sofia went on hoeing the dry field and tried to imagine the best name for the boy. Raul, she thought. She liked that name. One of the doctors who had looked after her in hospital had been called Raul. But it meant that in her mind, the name was already taken. She thought hard. Jorge, Abiliou, Rogiero, Bento, Nicolaus, Elliot . . . None of these suited him. She straightened her back again. None of the names she knew was good enough for him. There was nothing else for it, she'd have to invent her own name. She looked up into the sky. The white contour of the moon was visible. The moon would be full that evening.

'Moonboy,' she thought. That's what I'll call him.

A *Mupfana wa N'wheti*. The boy who had come walking out of the sun but really belonged with the moon. She laughed out loud at her own thoughts. Almost blushed, too. Now she missed not being able to talk to Rosa, who would have understood. But afterwards, if he had come back, she might not have left him alone. Sofia decided that the Moonboy would be one of the secrets she would not share with anyone. Not even with Rosa.

After about an hour she put the hoe down and went to have a drink of water from the bucket. It was kept in the little shed they used as a kitchen. Alfredo had stopped drawing in the sand and was looking at her. It meant that he wanted something to eat. Sofia gave him an orange and a piece of bread. She wasn't hungry—well, she was, but she must try to eat a little less than she usually did. She was becoming far too fat and if she didn't look out she'd get a really big bottom and big breasts, like Mrs Mukulela. She didn't want that, at least not for years and years.

She went into the hut and quietly pulled back the curtain to their room. Rosa was asleep. She was breathing through her open mouth. Sofia listened to her quick, shallow breaths, then tiptoed to the bed and put her hand on Rosa's forehead. It felt less hot than before. It's nothing serious, she told herself. There was no need for me to be scared.

On her way out of the hut, she caught sight of a plastic bag on the floor. It was where Rosa kept all her combs and creams and things. The temptation was too much for Sofia, who leaned on one crutch and used the other as a hook. She carried the bag next door and sat down on the only stool in the room. Then she took out the cream that made Rosa's face so shiny and started rubbing it into her own face. The cream had a lovely, mysterious smell. When she had finished, she put the jar back in the plastic bag. Rosa wouldn't notice.

She went out into the yard. The sun was still high in the sky. Mrs Mukulela had switched off her radio and gone inside. Sofia could hear her snoring. Mrs Mukulela always took a nap at this time of the day. You could set your watch by her—if you had one, that is. Sofia looked at her face in the piece of mirror glass. Her skin glowed. For a brief moment she could forget about her legs and believe that she was almost as good-looking as Rosa.

Then she hung the mirror on the wall again and turned to look at the road. Two women were walking along, both dressed in black and carrying large bundles of firewood on their heads.

No boy to be seen anywhere. It made her feel sad. She knew it was silly, but she couldn't help it. So, he had just been passing. Now he was gone for ever. Sofia was a person he had happened to ask about the way to his uncle's hut. He would have forgotten her as soon as he went out of sight down the slope.

Time passed.

Mrs Mukulela woke up from her nap and came out into her yard to splash water over her big body. Sofia thought she was like an elephant at a pool. During her long stay in hospital, when she had been fitted with her leg prostheses and was able to leave her bed, she had often gone to the sitting room in the evenings and watched the programs on the old black-and-white TV set. Once there had been a film about elephants and they had been splashing water about, just like Mrs Mukulela.

Sofia played for a while with Alfredo, and then she started preparing the evening meal. When Lydia came back, Sofia had put the corn cobs in to soak and had lit the fire. Lydia was tired. Faustino was hanging asleep on her back.

Lydia looked around.

'Where's Rosa?'

'She's ill in bed.'

'What, is she in pain?'

Lydia always became very worried when one of her children fell ill. Sofia understood why. Lydia feared losing another child.

'She's got a fever. But she feels less hot now than this morning.'

Lydia rushed into the hut but soon came out again.

'She's hardly got any temperature now,' she said. 'Rosa is running about too much in the evenings. It tires her out.'

Rosa didn't want anything to eat. She only wanted to sleep.

Lydia was tired after her long day at the *machamba*. They all went to bed early. Sofia was to stay at home from school the next day as well.

The moonlight shone in through the small window.

Sofia let her thoughts drift. Rosa was sleeping next to her on the floor. Moonboy had not returned. He had disappeared down the slope and maybe gone on to find his uncle's hut.

Sleep was pulling her in.

She put her hand over her stomach. The cold feeling in there, which had started when Rosa dropped the hoe and collapsed, was almost gone now. But not quite.

Somewhere in there was a place where her worries had settled.

Suddenly, she sat up in bed.

Something had tugged her out of her sleep. She listened. The night was silent—the only sound was the singing of the crickets.

Moonlight filled the room.

39

She had no idea why she did what she did then.

She sat up on the edge of her bed and strapped on her prostheses. Then she put on her body-wrap, grabbed her crutches and cautiously crossed the room where Lydia and the boys were sleeping. The door had been left ajar and she pushed at it gently. The moonlight was flowing over the village like a blue mist. She expected Lydia to wake at any moment, but she was deeply asleep.

Sofia went outside. It was as if she had stepped into a different world, not black night but blue.

Then she saw him.

He was standing motionless in the road. Sofia had no doubt.

It was the boy. Moonboy had returned.

FIVE

Just at that moment the moonlight seemed to change. It turned a brighter, more intense blue.

Sofia did not move. The boy in the road was motionless. Sofia couldn't see his face. She could feel her heart beat. Or was someone, somewhere, playing the drums? Was there a drummer inside her chest, playing a small blue drum?

She still did not move.

I'm dreaming, she said to herself. This isn't happening.

She tightened one hand hard round the handle of one of her crutches to convince herself that it was just air. In dreams everything one touched felt like air or very thin silk. But her crutch did not dissolve between her fingers like smoke or mist. She was really standing outside the hut in the moonlit night.

The boy had started to move and was coming closer to her.

He seemed to hover rather than walk. His footsteps made no noise. Sofia moved away from the door. Lydia might wake, one could never be sure. No one else had such sharp ears or slept so lightly. It was odd that she hadn't heard Sofia pass through the room. Or maybe she had, but thought that Sofia needed to go outside for a pee.

The boy had stopped again.

Still she could not make out his face. He had left the road close to one of Lydia's banana trees. Sofia took a few steps towards him. Now she could see his face. It really was her boy who had come back. She stopped and looked down at her feet. Her wrap was long enough. It was important that her legs were covered, even though the prostheses did not show up in the moonlight.

She was close to him now. He looked at her and smiled.

'I didn't think it was possible,' he said quietly.

Sofia thought she had never heard such a beautiful voice before. It sounded as if he might start singing any minute.

I'm so silly, she thought. He speaks like everyone else. I'll start blushing if I think about his voice as beautiful. Maybe it will show even in moonlight.

She was just about to say something when it came to her that she'd better get a little closer to him, or Lydia might hear them.

Just as she took a step forward, her legs and crutches got entangled and she fell. It was as if she had thrown herself at his feet.

All Sofia wanted was to die. She must get away, get back into the hut and to sleep. How she hated these legs that would never manage on their own. She'd break her crutches and throw them away. She'd spend the rest of her life crawling. That is, if she ever left the hut again.

Then she felt his hand on her arm.

'Are you all right?' he asked. Sofia didn't answer.

He helped her up. She breathed in the smell of his body: a mixture of sweat and soap. She liked it. The smell was strong but warm at the same time. Maybe he washes himself with moonsoap, she thought. Then she stopped herself short: now she was being silly again.

He handed her a crutch that she had dropped.

It doesn't matter any more, Sofia thought.

Nothing matters any more. Now he can see how it is with me. Soon he'll be gone.

She leaned over to brush the dust off her body-wrap, but in fact she was hitting her legs to punish them.

Her eyes filled with tears. Rosa should have been standing there, not me. I'm not good enough.

'Did you hurt yourself?' he asked.

Sofia didn't answer. She straightened her back but kept her eyes downcast, because she didn't want to look into his eyes.

'Are you all right?' he asked again. 'Are you hurt?'

'Why does he have to go on about it,' Sofia thought.

She suddenly felt she disliked him. So, he came through the moonlight to see her. He still didn't have to nag.

'I didn't find my uncle,' he said. 'But I'm sure he lives somewhere near here. In a hut with a window close to the ground.'

Now Sofia had to look at him. 'A window close to the ground? Why?'

'My uncle is an odd man. He likes lying on the ground and watching people.'

'How strange. Why?'

'He says that you get a better view if you see people the way a frog would.'

Sofia shook her head. She had forgotten by now that she had fallen over.

'Why just a frog?'

'I don't know. But he's always been rather odd.'

They both fell silent. Their talk seemed to have come to an end.

The boy moved his head. Sofia could see both his eyes

now. The light was so strong she even spotted a small scar under one of them.

'It was a bird,' he said.

Sofia didn't understand what he meant.

'A bird pecked me near my eye when I was little. I still remember it: a white bird with a yellow beak. Something had happened to it. Maybe it had hit a tree or its own image in a mirror. Anyway, it had knocked itself out and become confused. It flew straight at me. Its beak punctured my skin.'

'What happened to it afterwards?'

'The bird dropped to the ground. Dead.'

Was he really telling the truth? Sofia was amazed at his story. Maybe boys who stepped out of the moonlight had their own special way of speaking.

'Why are you standing in the road at night?' she asked.

'I was leaving. But then I thought you might hear when I stopped walking.'

What did that mean? How could she have heard someone who moved so soundlessly along the road? How could she have picked up the sound of a pair of feet that had stopped moving?

She looked at his feet. His trousers had been cut off unevenly at the bottom. Sofia would never have shortened them so carelessly. He was barefoot.

But he could be right after all, she thought. There was

45

something that pulled me out of my sleep. Perhaps I heard something I no longer remember.

Then she recalled what he had said first of all: 'I didn't think it was possible.'

'What did you mean then? What did you think wasn't possible?' she asked.

'That you might hear that I was here.'

This time Sofia did blush. She couldn't avoid it any more. Furious with herself, she thought it might well be even more obvious in moonlight than in sunshine.

Right now, the moon was not her friend. But then no one, nothing, was her friend.

'What's you name?' the boy asked.

Sofia thought quickly that she ought to say that her name was Rosa. Then, if the boy came back the next day, she could ask Rosa to speak to him. The fever would surely be gone by then. As soon as he saw Rosa, Sofia's far too lovely sister, he would forget for ever that girl who had been stumbling and falling over her plastic legs and crutches, and blushing so much that the moonlight itself had turned bright red.

'Sofia,' she said. 'What's your name?'

'I don't know.'

There's something wrong with his head, Sofia thought. Everyone knows his own name.

'I often change my name,' he went on. 'But today

I haven't been able to make up my mind.'

'Don't you have a real name?'

'All my names are real names. It's just that I like changing them. You don't eat the same food every day. You don't wear the same clothes. Why stick to the same name?'

Sofia began to think she should be frightened by this boy. Lydia had told her to be very careful if she met people who behaved oddly. You could never be sure what they might do or say next.

'You give me a name,' the boy said. 'I feel quite naked in the moonlight without a name.'

Sofia stared at him. What was that he had said? That he was naked? She looked down, as if he really had been standing there without any clothes on.

'Sergio,' she said.

'Sergio? Why?'

Sofia really didn't want to answer. Once, someone called Sergio used to play with her and Maria, but he had only lived for eight years. Then he got malaria and died. Afterwards his mother had been with Lydia many evenings, weeping.

When Lydia and Sergio's mother wept together, it was like the sea hitting rocks and etching lines into their surfaces. The grief of all mothers for their dead children marked the two women's faces.

Maria was a deep fold on Lydia's forehead.

The deepest fold of them all.

But Sofia did not say anything about all this. Just that Sergio was a beautiful name.

The boy laughed.

Sofia thought it sounded like water dripping and rustling over a roof. If someone had asked where she got that idea from, she would not have been able to say. She just knew. Moonboy's laughter sounded like the rustling of water.

'There, I've got a name,' the boy said. 'Now I don't need to be afraid any more.'

Sofia did not find out what he was afraid of. At least not there and then.

She started. The door to the hut was pushed open.

At first she thought Lydia might have woken up and heard them talking. Then she saw it was Rosa. She moved only a few steps away from the hut, crouched down and peed.

Sofia turned around.

The boy had disappeared. The road was empty. Sofia could not understand how he got away so fast. She looked up towards the moon, but he wasn't there either.

Rosa stood up. To her surprise, she saw Sofia outside.

'What are you doing?' she asked.

'I couldn't sleep.' Sofia walked towards Rosa. 'Do you feel better now?'

Rosa nodded. But Sofia noticed that Rosa was trembling.

'I don't understand what's the matter with me,' she said.

Sofia realised that the cold feeling had come back to her stomach.

She looked towards the road once more. Her Moonboy was not there.

SIX

❧

Rosa really did feel better the next day. She got up as usual in the morning. The fever had gone and her forehead felt cool, but she was still tired and had no appetite.

Sofia kept an eye on her sister. The chill in Sofia's stomach had partly gone away, but a bad feeling was in there somewhere. Rosa washed just as slowly and carefully as usual. Afterwards she would normally carry on for ages in front of the mirror, rubbing in creams and fixing her hair in different ways. This day was no different and Sofia thought it was a good sign. Surely nothing could be seriously wrong with Rosa for as long as she still cared how she looked?

Just before Lydia set out for the *machamba* with Faustino on her back, she and Rosa quarrelled briefly. Lydia told Rosa to walk to the health centre, which was some four kilometres away from the village, along the road to Boane, but Rosa didn't want to go.

'You were ill yesterday,' Lydia said crossly. 'So, maybe you'd better let the doctor examine you to make sure there's nothing wrong with you—something that might hit you again.'

'There's no need.'

'Why not?'

'Because I'm fine today.'

Sofia was washing herself while she listened to them. She could hear that Lydia was upset. Rosa was too independent of her mother to hold back from arguing.

'But what if you're unwell again tomorrow?' Lydia insisted.

'I won't be.'

'How do you know?'

Round and round the argument went. Irritation glowed like embers not quite ready to flare into flames. In the end Lydia gave up and went off towards the *machamba* with Faustino on her back and the hoe in her hand.

Rosa sat down in the shade.

'Thanks for doing my weeding yesterday,' she said.

'The weeds aren't yours, they're ours. Besides, you weren't well.'

'Thanks anyway.'

Sofia was standing with one elbow resting on her crutch.

'Hey, what were you up to last night?' Rosa said. 'I got the idea you were talking to somebody.'

'Who would that be?'

'I don't know, that's why I'm asking.'

Sofia quickly weighed in her mind the reasons for and against telling Rosa about the boy. He had vanished when Rosa came out for her pee, so in a way it was her fault that he had gone. But there was no point in being angry with Rosa. After all, no one could help needing a pee.

Anyway, Rosa did not seem particularly interested to hear the answer. She stood up and stretched her arms in the air.

'I'll go round to the shop,' she said. 'Maybe Hassan has got in some new magazines. It would be nice to check them out.'

Hassan's shop was on the far side of the school, near the ruined house that used to be called the 'Soldier's House'. Sofia had no idea who the soldier really was and she had never met him. Lydia had told her that he had been famous for his courage during the war against the Portuguese. That war had been waged long before Sofia was born. When the war was over he had built a house in their village. It seemed that he had never quite understood that the war was over. Sometimes he would dream of foreign soldiers surrounding him and start firing his rifle in the middle of the night. Once, he had shot a bullet right through the wall of a nearby hut and hit the foot of a man who'd been sleeping in there. Then all the villagers had gone to visit old Cossa, the village chief, to complain about the soldier. A few weeks later he left in a rage, but first he tore his house down because he didn't want anyone else to live in it. He said a curse over it as well and even though it was a good site near the road, nobody dared to build on it.

Nobody, that is, except Hassan.

Hassan was half Indian and wasn't worried at all by stories about old black soldiers and their curses. Anyway, he wasn't much of an Indian either. Rosa said that he claimed the blood in his veins was a terrific mixture: Arabic, Greek, Indian, African, German, American, Turkish and Russian. This made it very difficult to work out what kind of a person he really was. His skin was pale brown, so he looked like an Indian merchant. He had set up his shop next to the ruin and it had become a real meeting-place, especially for young boys who wanted to talk to girls, and for girls who wanted to talk to boys. Rosa had tried to tempt Sofia to come with her to the shop many times, but Sofia always refused. She thought that everyone would stare at her plastic legs and her crutches, and see nothing else.

Rosa had told her that sometimes Hassan would switch on his radio. When there was music on they'd all dance. Sofia couldn't dance.

Not being able to dance was her greatest sorrow in life.

When other people danced and she watched, knowing that she couldn't join them, the feeling that she no longer wanted to live came to her more strongly than at other bad times.

Lydia didn't like Rosa going to the shop. She had heard enough about what happened in the dark behind that shop.

Rosa took no notice of what Lydia said and went along anyway. Apart from the boys, she was very keen on the magazines that Hassan got from a cousin of his who lived in the city. These magazines could be several years out of date, but it didn't matter. Rosa wanted to see the pictures of people in smart clothes. Many of them were white, but Rosa didn't mind. She knew she was beautiful, and that was all that mattered to her.

Rosa went into the hut. When she came out again she was wearing one of Sofia's shawls draped over her shoulders. 'Please, can I borrow it?'

Sofia nodded. She liked it when Rosa borrowed her clothes. It somehow felt as if she herself was going to Hassan's shop.

Rosa left and Sofia was alone with Alfredo.

Suddenly, the day ahead seemed very long. She wished that she'd been in school instead, but it would be three more days before school opened again. Tomorrow was Saturday and then there was Sunday. First thing on Monday morning she would pack her rucksack and set out for school again.

She tried to think of what to do. The laundry? No, Lydia had dealt with that last Saturday. The pile of dirty clothes was still not that big. Tidy the hut? Rosa had done that the day before she fell ill. She looked around. There was Mrs Mukulela, mending one of her huge bras. Sofia burst out laughing, because it looked like two big white baskets held together by a strip of material. Mr Temba had already left for the market to sell his baskets.

She thought about the boy in the road. She had given him a name. Sergio. Now he had gone and taken that name with him. He might at least come and give the name back, Sofia thought. It was just his on loan, and people who have things on loan should give them back— even if it's just a name.

The day passed and Lydia came back. She was tired.

'Where's Rosa?' she asked. 'Did she go to the health centre after all?'

'I don't know,' Sofia said.

That wasn't quite true, but not a complete lie either. Rosa might not have gone to Hassan's shop.

Lydia seemed to have read her thoughts.

'Don't bother saying any more,' she said. 'An answer like that means that Rosa's gone to see Hassan and look through his magazines. They just give her a lot of good-for-nothing ideas.'

They cooked a meal.

By the time they sat down to eat, Rosa had still not come back.

'This disease they're talking about,' Lydia said suddenly. 'It frightens me. I fear for Rosa and the life she's leading.'

'I'm frightened, too,' Sofia said.

Lydia sat down on the ground and pulled her legs up under her. Faustino was sleepily hanging on her arm.

'Everybody seems to have something to say about the disease, but nobody knows what it's really like,' Lydia said. 'You know something, don't you? You're going to school, so they must have taught you about it.'

Sofia realised for the first time that nobody at school talked about that disease. It was really strange. All she knew, she had learnt in the hospital from Deolinda, who had been in the bed next to her own. Until the morning she died.

Sophia tried to explain to Lydia. It wasn't exactly easy, because she had to mention things she usually didn't speak to her mother about, like what happened when a man and a woman were together. Lydia listened attentively.

When Sofia had finished, Lydia shook her head and sighed.

'Rosa simply has to stop running about with boys at night,' she said.

Faustino and Alfredo had fallen asleep. Mr Temba had returned from the market and was sitting outside his hut. He was singing, which meant that he had sold a lot of baskets and earned enough money to buy a bottle of wine to bring back home. He often sang quite rude songs. If he went too far, Lydia would shout at him, telling him to be quiet. But tonight she didn't seem to hear him.

The fire had almost gone out when Rosa emerged out of the darkness.

By then Lydia was asleep, but Rosa's footsteps woke her up. She immediately started telling Rosa off. Sofia walked away down the road because she didn't like having to listen. She already knew what Lydia would say and how Rosa would answer. Sofia agreed with Rosa most of the time, but not now. What upset Lydia was really important. Rosa ought not to be going out in the evenings such a lot, and she was crazy to keep chasing new boyfriends, just because she hoped the next one might be better fun.

That disease was lurking out there in the darkness. It was invisible, but cunning and ready to attack anyone and everyone.

Sofia was walking alone on the road.

The sky was covered in low clouds. She could hardly see a single step ahead, and at each step, before she put her foot down, she struck the ground hard with her crutch to scare off snakes. Just a few days ago, they had spotted a black cobra slithering across their yard only a few paces from where Alfredo was playing.

Then she stopped and held her breath. The crickets were singing out there in the dark, and from somewhere came the sound of a woman laughing. A little later, she heard a dog barking. Rosa's and Lydia's voices were out of earshot.

Moonboy came into Sofia's mind. Now that she was alone, she felt she could think about things that she wouldn't have dared to imagine when other people were around. What would it be like to be close to Moonboy? What if he held her and he was naked? What would it feel like when he touched her, and when she explored his body?

Rosa had told her about encounters like that, and the feeling of truly wanting a man to be with you.

Standing there in the road, Sofia suddenly realised that she knew what Rosa had been talking about. She wasn't sure what to call the sensation: tingling? glowing? It was utterly new to her body. She noticed that her palms had become moist with sweat.

Someone came stumbling along the road. It was Mr Temba, and he distracted her.

Mr Temba was very drunk and probably on his way to a hut where he knew a woman would be waiting for him. He didn't notice Sofia, just tottered past her and disappeared into the darkness.

Sofia started to walk back home then. Rosa and Lydia had stopped arguing. They were both trying to put out the last dying embers of the fire.

Sofia waited until they had gone inside the hut.

She looked around. Moonboy wasn't there.

SEVEN

The next day turned out to be a bad day, in every way. Sofia woke at dawn and discovered she had wet the bed. It was fairly rare, but it did happen often enough for her to worry about the possibility that it might. She didn't know exactly why she did it, but a doctor had explained to her that it was one of the consequences of her injuries from the landmine accident. She accepted this, but still she felt just as bad every time it happened.

She felt ashamed. After all, little kids peed themselves, but not young people who were practically grown-ups.

This was enough to make it a bad day, right from the start.

It became much, much worse when they discovered that during the night someone had stolen Lydia's big iron cooking pot. The pot was kept in the shed where they prepared most of their food.

Lydia herself discovered that it had gone. At first, she became very angry. Furious, she went round to their neighbours' houses to ask if anyone had noticed thieves about last night. Neither Mrs Mukulela nor Mr Temba had seen or heard anything. Besides, Mr Temba had actually been out all night. Sofia could confirm that. He said that when he came back home later on, all had been quiet. Sofia asked herself, under her breath—of course she didn't say it out aloud—if Mr Temba would have spotted an elephant if one had been lumbering around that night.

There was no getting away from it: the pot had disappeared. Lydia's anger was slowly displaced by sadness, and then tired resignation.

Now and then Sofia would wonder about what went on inside her mother's head. Lydia's moods could be violent, sometimes for no reason. This time though, Sofia understood very well. It had taken Lydia a long time to save the money for the cooking pot. She had put aside every penny she could spare, and had been radiantly happy on the day when she walked back from Boane with the pot balanced on her head.

So this day could not have had a more awful start, for sure.

But it got worse still. Just when Lydia was ready to set out for the *machamba*, much later than usual, Alfredo chased one of Mrs Mukulela's hens out into the road. Normally cars were rare, but just then a heavily laden truck came rumbling along. The hen had no idea how to cope with traffic and managed to get itself run over by one of the truck's front wheels.

By now Mrs Mukulela had realised something was up and came hurrying along to find out what was going on. Lydia smacked Alfredo, who began to cry. Then a row broke out between Lydia, Mrs Mukulela and the truck driver.

Sofia had never heard anything quite like it. True, not a week passed without Lydia and Mrs Mukulela quarrelling from time to time. But just as often they were the best of friends, chatting and laughing happily together. This time though, a third person was involved. Because the truck driver was there, the whole argument turned into a huge row of a kind quite new to Sofia. The driver was a big, fat man, with large patches of sweat staining his shirt.

At first, he just listened to Lydia and Mrs Mukulela screaming at one another. After a while he decided to put forward his own point of view, but it did him no good. Both women turned on him and loudly told him off for driving far too fast. This started off a real racket that went on for the best part of half an hour, and meantime quite a crowd had gathered in the road. People took sides for and against, and then switched right round when they felt they'd heard a good point. Still, gradually everybody seemed to agree that the driver had been speeding. Besides, it was getting too hot to bother. In the end, Lydia was big-hearted enough to give the driver a drink of water before he drove off.

The lorry disappeared in a cloud of dust. The crowd scattered. Mrs Mukulela calmed down and decided to eat the dead hen for supper.

If this awful day had been like an empty sack in the morning, Sofia thought, by now it must be filled to the top. It would have no room for any more bad things. This must be it.

She was wrong.

Just before Lydia finally got ready to leave, Sofia remembered that she had to ask for money. On Monday she had to bring the school fee for that term. This was very important. Pupils who didn't pay the fee in time could be expelled from school.

Sofia knew full well that this was a bad time to ask Lydia. Money was always a sensitive subject, because they never had enough. On the other hand, she knew that Lydia was keen for her to go to school, so she steeled herself to speak up.

Lydia looked at her, not wanting to understand.

'You got money for school last month, a lot of money, 50,000 *meticais*,' she said.

'That was for books.'

Lydia shook her head.

'I haven't got any money. Can't this wait until my tomatoes are ripe enough to be sold at the market?'

'I must bring the money on Monday,' Sofia mumbled. She felt sorry for them both. Why did they have to be so poor?

'Couldn't you have told me earlier?' Lydia said.

'I forgot.'

'Forgot! How could you forget something like this?'

Lydia sat down and put her hoe away.

Sofia stood close by, leaning on her crutches. She was thinking about all the times she'd been in town, walking about and looking at the displays in the shop windows and on the market stalls. The amounts on the price-tags seemed unbelievable. Still, there had been people everywhere who could afford these things. Some of them were young, even her age, but they carried large wads of cash. They could easily spend in a moment more than Lydia could earn after days and days of back-breaking labour on the *machamba*.

Sofia needed 30,000 *meticais*. She had seen pairs of shoes in town shops costing 3,000,000 *meticais*.

'I don't know what to do,' Lydia said. 'There's no point trying to sell unripe tomatoes. No money in that.' She sighed.

'I shall have to borrow the money from Mrs Mukulela,' she went on. 'Or maybe Mr Temba. There's no other way.'

'Let me ask,' Sofia said. She knew only too well that Lydia detested having to borrow money.

'No, I'll do it,' Lydia replied, straightening her back. 'It's humiliating, but it's my job and not yours. I'm your mother, and it's my responsibility.'

She rose, picked up the hoe, patted Faustino to settle him more comfortably into place on her back, and started walking.

Sofia kept looking after her as she walked away.

She felt very sorry for Lydia. She had always been poor, and had never known where the money would come from next. Today someone had made things even worse for her by stealing her cooking pot.

What was it like to be Lydia? What made her able to carry on? Sofia asked herself these questions and behind them was her own certainty that when she was a grown-up, she didn't want to live like Lydia.

Now Lydia had disappeared out of sight.

Alfredo was sitting in the shade of the hut, playing with some pieces of wood. Sofia thought he needed cheering up. Lydia had not really been cross when she smacked him. It was just that she had feared for him when she saw him so near the heavy truck. He could have been run over.

There was no need to fret about the hen. It was just a silly old bird, or it would have scuttled out of harm's way in time. Besides, just imagine how much the tasty supper would please Mrs Mukulela.

Sofia looked around.

Where was Rosa? Sofia hadn't seen her while the big row was going on. This was odd and unlike Rosa. She liked it when unusual things happened. Sofia went to look inside the hut, but it was empty. Maybe Rosa had set out for Hassan's shop after all.

Then she saw her.

Rosa was sitting in the shade of a tree that grew on the border between their land and Mr Temba's. Sofia screwed up her eyes to see her better. Sometimes Rosa went off on her own because she wanted to be left in peace, maybe to think about some trouble or other in her love-life. Mostly she got over it quite quickly.

So, what was the problem this time? A row with someone she'd been going out with? But no, something told Sofia that Rosa had a different reason for sitting under that tree.

Sofia walked over to her. Rosa had been crying and tears were still gleaming on her cheeks. Tears could look beautiful, even when they meant real sorrow.

Sofia came closer.

'What's the matter?' she asked.

'Nothing.'

'Come on. You wouldn't cry just for nothing.'

'I don't feel well.'

'Are you hurting anywhere?'

'No. I'm so very tired. That's all.'

The cold feeling was creeping back into Sofia's stomach. She held on to the tree trunk and slowly lowered herself to sit next to Rosa.

Rosa was sad.

Maybe frightened, too. Sofia wasn't sure, but she, too, felt afraid. Her memories of Deolinda were coming back. Rosa and Deolinda seemed so similar, even though Rosa was sitting under a tree rather than lying in a hospital bed.

'Maybe Lydia is right,' Sofia said.

'How do you mean, right?'

'Right about you going out too much, too late.'

'So what's supposed to be so dangerous about going off to look at magazines in a shop?'

Sofia was taken aback. She didn't know how to answer.

Actually, she did, but couldn't think of a way to start speaking about the difficult things. Like the dangerous disease. Or how important it was to be careful when you were in love.

It might be too late already.

67

At this thought, Sofia stiffened. Rosa was looking straight at her.

'What's wrong with you?' she asked.

'Nothing.'

Rosa got up.

'I'm going indoors to lie down for a bit.'

'Use my bed if you like.'

Rosa didn't answer. She walked slowly over to the hut and disappeared through the door.

When Sofia popped her head in a little later, Rosa was asleep. She had chosen to lie on the straw mat next to the bed.

EIGHT

The bad day took a long time to end, but at last the evening arrived.

Lydia was exhausted when she returned from the *machamba*. Anxiety made her stiffen when Sofia told her that Rosa had felt tired and slept for most of the day. Sofia didn't mention that Rosa had been in tears, sitting alone under a tree. There was no need to worry Lydia too much just then. All the same she hesitated, for surely she ought to share all her concerns with Lydia? Lydia never seemed to hold back from asking Sofia questions.

Sofia simply couldn't make up her mind about what to do.

This uncertainty was only too familiar. It was one of her characteristics that she liked least: she always thought of more than one way of doing things, so that it took her for ever to work out what she really wanted.

Lydia and Sofia prepared the supper together.

While the rice was cooking, Lydia went into the hut. Sofia listened at the door. She could hear Rosa's and Lydia's quiet voices, but couldn't make out the words.

When Lydia came back out, Sofia just managed to step away from the door, but couldn't move quickly enough on her crutches. Lydia fixed her stern eyes on Sofia.

'So, you were listening!'

Sofia shook her head, but Lydia didn't believe her. Still, she said nothing more.

They had rice with vegetables for supper.

'We have enough to last us until Tuesday,' Lydia said. 'After that I don't know what we will do.'

Lydia and Sofia, and probably Alfredo, too, sniffed the air for the smell of roasting chicken coming from Mrs Mukulela's house.

'Maybe I could take in some more sewing,' Sofia said, to cheer Lydia up. 'Maybe the Milagre family has some clothes for me. It's been months since I had anything from them, and they always pay on the nail.'

Lydia shook her head.

'You haven't got the time,' she said. 'You've got your schoolwork to do every day.'

'I could do my sewing in the evenings.'

'You won't be able to see well enough. It's getting dark by then.'

Sofia knew that Lydia was right. The sewing machine was kept in the hut. When the light was poor, Sofia might easily make mistakes that would upset her customers. Angry customers might well refuse to pay.

Their talk died away. After a while Lydia straightened her back. 'I can't bear any more gloomy thoughts tonight,' she said. 'What's the point of living without a good laugh now and then? None. Well, one laugh a day, anyhow.'

Then Lydia went on to tell Sofia about Mrs Inocencia, who lived in a tumbledown cottage near the *machamba*.

Mrs Inocencia liked her beer. Sometimes she wasn't entirely sober when she turned up at dawn to work in the fields. No one thought any worse of her for that. They were all fond of her and didn't blame her for the evenings when she took a drink or two more than was good for her.

Mrs Inocencia had been married twice, and both her husbands had died in accidents. The first husband had fallen off his tractor on his way to the market, and the second one had drowned in the river one night. He had stumbled crossing a bridge in the dark. When her first husband died, Mrs Inocencia mourned him for more than a year. She only stopped crying after she met the man who was to become her second husband. He fell off the bridge when they had been married for only a few months, and Mrs Inocencia began crying again. She also took to drinking beer to drown her sorrows.

71

'She was a little wobbly this morning,' Lydia said. 'But she was keen to show us that she could do her work all right. So she swung her hoe with a will. Trouble was, she was trying a bit too hard—she hit herself on the head and fell over!' Lydia laughed out loud. 'One shouldn't laugh at other people's misery,' she said afterwards. 'But maybe right now, there's someone else who thinks I'm funny.'

Mrs Mukulela suddenly emerged out of the darkness carrying a dish. In it were pieces of roasted run-over hen.

'Where's Rosa?' she asked, curious as ever.

'Oh, she's here. She's stopped running around at night,' Lydia replied sharply.

Next, Mrs Mukulela looked around for Alfredo, who had quickly crawled away to hide behind Sofia's back. He was scared of Mrs Mukulela, because he thought she was still angry with him.

'I've brought a few bits of chicken for Alfredo,' Mrs Mukulela said. 'After all, I've got him to thank for my nice supper.'

Sofia gave Alfredo a push to make him come out of hiding. Soon he was wolfing down the chicken, which tasted much nicer than rice and vegetables. Besides, Alfredo was always hungry, however much he ate.

Lydia got out one of the stools for Mrs Mukulela, who sat down heavily.

'My tooth hurts,' she complained. 'I bit too hard on a chicken bone.'

'Why don't you ask Mr Temba to have a look at it?' Lydia asked. 'He's good. Once he pulled one of my teeth out.'

Mrs Mukulela took offence at that.

'I'd never even think of letting that man look into my mouth,' she exclaimed. 'Why, he might tear my tongue out. Or at least threaten to. That is, unless I . . .'

She didn't finish her sentence, but there was no need to. Sofia, for one, had no trouble filling in the missing bit: '. . . spend the night with him.'

At that precise moment, Mr Temba stepped into the circle round the fire. He always moved soundlessly.

He had an old hat on his head, kept in place with a scarf. 'I hope I'm not disturbing you,' he said and bowed, first to Lydia and then, even more politely, to Mrs Mukulela. Suspicious of him or not, still she wriggled flirtatiously on her stool.

Mr Temba was carrying a bundle.

'The wind is rising now,' he said. 'Tonight a "hats-fly-away" wind will be blowing from the south. Better be prepared, I thought, and tied my hat firmly in place. I must tell you that I inherited this hat from one of my

73

uncles. His name was Justino. His story was that he had found the hat on the road to Namascha. Now, I suspect that he stole it. Be that as it may, Justino was a very nice man and didn't make a habit of stealing things. Only now and then.'

Mrs Mukulela snorted. 'Surely it would have been better to keep your hat at home, if it's supposed to be getting so windy.'

'Hats are like people,' Mr Temba said, sounding wise. 'Hats don't like being left behind on their own.'

By now Lydia was gurgling with laughter. Sofia had burst out laughing, too. Lydia always made others share her own pleasure at a joke.

Mr Temba handed his bundle over to Sofia.

'I've brought some shirts that need mending,' he said. 'Please, feel free to say No if you haven't got the time.'

Lydia and Sofia looked at each other.

Now Sofia didn't have to ask the Milagres or anybody else for work. Mr Temba had come to them out of the dark night, as if he had heard them talk about running out of food.

'Shirts don't last nowadays, not like they used to,' Mr Temba said regretfully.

'That might well have something to do with your

growing so fat,' Mrs Mukulela told him.

Mr Temba untied his scarf so that he could doff his hat to her.

'As you have, too, my dear,' he said.

He should not have said that.

Mrs Mukulela rose from her seat. The stool creaked when she got up. She walked away without saying a word.

'I cannot understand that woman,' Mr Temba said sadly. 'I've offered to marry her, but she keeps refusing me.'

'You must be patient,' Lydia told him. 'You never know, maybe sooner or later she'll accept you.'

Mr Temba sat down on the stool.

Sofia felt happy when she looked into his dark, kind face and bright eyes. There were times she felt he was the man she liked best of all. This did not mean that she found it any easier to imagine him being with Lydia, and maybe even being the father of her little brother.

Mr Temba seemed thoughtful. 'The moon is really beautiful tonight,' he said.

He looked at Sofia as he said that.

At once she wondered if, after all, he had noticed her in the road that night, when he had come walking on unsteady legs to meet up with a woman somewhere.

They stayed silent for a while. Everyone was deep in thought. At first Sofia was thinking about the shirts, and how the family wouldn't have to go without food just yet. Then she thought about Rosa, but she shied away from more worrying.

After that, she thought about Moonboy for a long time.

Surely he'd never come back. She looked into the fire, trying to see the features of his face in the flames. But the fire did not give away any secrets. This was different from how it used to be only a year or so ago, when Sofia had been convinced that the fire would always tell her the secrets she wanted to know. Now it seemed to have changed. Maybe she was becoming too old.

A sudden gust of wind made the fire flare up. Mr Temba grabbed hold of his hat.

'There's the wind coming now,' he said. 'The hat-stealing wind from the south that causes trouble wherever it blows.'

He got up and bowed to Lydia, still holding on to his hat with one hand. Then he disappeared into the dark night.

Sofia untied the bundle of shirts. Most of the mending seemed to be frayed collars and cuffs. It wouldn't take her long.

The last shirt she unpacked was blue.

Suddenly Sofia remembered something Lydia had told her when she was little. Why should it have come back to her just now? If you were longing to see someone, Lydia had said, then that person would come if you put a blue ribbon in the road when the moon was full. Sofia's heart started pounding. How could she have forgotten?

But she couldn't put Mr Temba's shirt in the road. It might get trodden on, or stolen. What if Mr Temba discovered what she'd done? He wouldn't give her his shirts to mend again, that much was sure. If it had become very dirty, he might demand payment for it.

Sofia tried to work out what to do.

Were there any blue ribbons in her sewing kit? No, definitely not.

Lydia rose and lifted Alfredo into her arms. He had fallen asleep by the fire. Faustino was already sleeping in the hut.

'I'm so tired,' Lydia said. 'Still, not to worry. We've had a few good laughs tonight.'

'I'll watch the fire until it goes out,' Sofia said.

Now she was on her own.

She kept staring at Mr Temba's blue shirt. An idea had come into her head, but it frightened her. How could she even think about it? To cut a strip off the shirt! Did she really believe in that old fairytale of Lydia's?

This kind of thing is simply not done, she told herself.

Besides, it's childish and I'm practically a grown-up. No way would I believe that putting a blue ribbon in the road can make someone come to me.

She looked up at the night sky.

The full moon was glowing. It was like a distant lamp, shining with a strong, bluish light.

She got up and went into the hut. Lydia had already fallen asleep.

Sofia kept her scissors in one of the drawers under the sewing machine. She felt for them carefully and tiptoed back outside with them.

Lydia woke up for a moment.

'Aren't you going to bed?' she mumbled.

'I forgot the shirts,' Sofia replied.

Lydia mumbled something else, but it was inaudible. Then she turned over on her straw mat. Faustino squeaked a little in his sleep.

Once she was back outside, Sofia tried to talk sense to herself. How could she imagine cutting a piece of material from Mr Temba's shirt?

But it was too late. She had already made up her mind and started blowing on the fire to make it glow more brightly. Then she cut a strip from the middle of the back of the blue shirt. She hoped she would be able to stitch it so that the cut wouldn't show.

She went out to the road.

The cicadas were singing. A dog barked a couple of times in the distance.

At the place where the boy had been standing, Sofia placed the blue ribbon on the ground. She looked up at the moon for the last time and then walked towards the hut.

In the doorway she turned and stood listening.

The night was still.

Mr Temba's wind had not come after all.

NINE

◎

That night Sofia had a dream. When she woke, she still remembered it in detail.

The moonlight was very bright, like a blue flame reaching down from the dark sky towards her face.

Sofia was standing in the middle of the road. The strip of blue material had disappeared. The whole roadway had turned blue. When she bent down and grabbed a handful of gravel, the blue grains trickled between her fingers.

The gravel was warm. A warm sensation flowed through her whole body.

Up there in the night sky the moon was swinging from side to side, like a lantern in the wind.

It was Mr Temba's wind, the kind that swept up people's hats and carried them off to a secret land where all lost hats and caps and berets lived.

In her dream, Sofia laughed at her own fantasy.

The air that came out of her mouth was blue. She looked down at her hand, which was transparent but shifting and glittering, as if her body had turned into the sea. She sensed that warm water was flowing through her. She felt a tremendous joy.

She must find Rosa, and Lydia, too, in order to share this lovely blue night with them. Then she realised that she was waiting for someone.

The boy. She looked around. The blue landscape was empty.

She felt afraid now. Maybe he would never come?

She looked down and pulled at the length of fabric wrapped around her hips. Her legs were not blue. They looked just the same as usual: brown, scratched plastic, cracked in places. She let the cloth fall back. Her crutches had not changed either.

The flowing, warm feeling inside her suddenly grew colder.

She felt certain about the meaning of this. He would not come and be tempted to join her inside her dream world. Or was it really a dream? Maybe she was awake all the time? She truly did not know.

Then she heard a sound from somewhere not too far away.

She could not work out where it came from. She listened intently, and started when something came flying at her through the air. A night bird? She saw it coming close and it was Mr Temba's hat, but with wings and a beak. It was whizzing around and around her. She tried to shoo it away. Suddenly it was gone.

Then she heard the sound again.

She began walking. The sound was her own singing, she realised, but not from her mouth. The sound came from her fingers. Her fingers were singing.

The blue gravel was very soft underfoot. She was sinking. Then moving through water.

She started composing a poem in her head.

When she turned to look back, she saw that her footsteps had left imprints of words in the blue sand. She had written something as she walked. This was what she read in the sand:

> *Sofia is in the blue night and love is blue.*
> *When Mr Temba's hat comes flying along,*
> *it brings a message:*
> *'Love is blue'.*

She found the poem very odd. Had she really thought it up herself?

Then she saw him. Moonboy.

He was walking along the road towards her, smiling and holding Mr Temba's hat in his hand. She searched her memory for his name and felt frightened, because if she had forgotten the name she had given him, he would walk past without seeing her. Desperately, she tried and tried to remember. It was like rushing around inside the dark hut, looking for something she had to have but could not find.

The boy was coming closer. Her heart almost stopped beating. Where had she hidden his name?

Then it came to her. Sergio.

The boy stopped. He smelt of cinnamon.

She let go of her crutches, but they didn't fall to the ground. Instead they turned into legs and ran away. Legs without a body.

Sofia immediately began to worry. The boy might think her peculiar. But he just stood there, quite still, and looked straight at her.

The sensation of warmth came back, and waves of blue water were tumbling inside her body.

The boy suddenly began to take his clothes off.

First his shirt. Its collar was frayed. Then Sofia said, 'I'll mend it.'

The boy didn't answer. He was taking his trousers off. One knee was torn. It looked just like the tear on

83

Alfredo's trousers that Sofia had mended a few days ago.

Now the boy was almost naked, apart from his under-pants. He was smiling at her.

Sofia nodded. It seemed to be very important that she should nod just at that moment.

The boy took off his last piece of clothing. Sofia had closed her eyes, but it didn't help. She saw what she saw anyway.

Then he touched her.

She felt his body against hers. Smelt his cinnamon scent. She realised that he was untying the length of fabric from around her hips. She had nothing on underneath, nothing but the straps holding on her legs. He took off her blouse. Now she was naked. She kept her eyes closed all the time.

But she dared to touch him, though hesitantly at first. She caressed his neck, his shoulders, his chest. Then lower down, where she really wanted to go.

Sofia touched him, held him firmly and felt his hand at the same time finding its way in between her legs. The sensation almost overpowered her. The cinnamon scent hung heavily in the air around them.

Then they slipped down to lie together in the road. It hurt when he pushed inside her, but not badly. Most of all, Sofia was afraid that she would wake up. She clung to him as if in that way she could cling to her dream. She feared that it would come apart and let reality back in through the cracks.

Her whole body had turned to warm water. They were floating about at sea, rocking from side to side.

Afterwards he helped her up. They dressed, and he stood there looking at her as if nothing had happened.

'What's your name?' he asked.

'Sofia.'

'What was the name you gave me?'

'Sergio.'

He smiled and said, 'Please, can I have another one?'

Sofia thought hard. She wanted to give him a name that he would like at once.

'Evaristou?'

'No, it's too long.'

'Zé.'

'I like that. It's much better. Zé. That's good. But now I must go.'

Sofia didn't want to ask him, but she had to.

'Will you be back?'

At that precise moment she opened her eyes. The memory of her dream was with her at once. But she did not know what his answer had been. Would he be back? She had no idea. Her dream had ended, there and then, as if someone had slammed a door shut.

Sofia lay still in the dark.

From the floor next to her bed she could hear Rosa's breathing. Sofia reached out a hand and patted her sister's hair. She noticed that Rosa was sweating, but that was no reason for worrying. Rosa often got sweaty during the night.

Sofia tried to get a feel for how much time was left before dawn—until Mrs Mukulela's rooster started its usual noise. She decided there was not long to wait. Soon the cock would crow.

The dream was still on her mind. She touched her body, sniffed her fingers. The scent of cinnamon lingered.

The cock started crowing.

When the light had grown stronger, Sofia got up and dressed.

Rosa woke. 'I'm feeling much better today,' she said and sat up.

Sofia thought that all her worries were over then. There was nothing wrong with Rosa. She just had to stay at home in the evening more often.

Sofia went outside. Lydia was getting the fire going. She looked up and saw Sofia.

'You seem in a good mood this morning. What's happened?' she asked.

Instead of answering, Sofia walked out in the road.

The strip of blue material was still there. She picked it up and hid it inside her skirt.

She still didn't know for sure if what had happened during the night had been nothing but a dream.

TEN

It was Sunday morning.

Just after ten o'clock, Lydia and Rosa set out for church. They took the two little boys with them. The church was a rickety white-limed house, built of bricks and covered by a tatty straw roof.

Sofia had decided to miss out on church and visit one of her secret places instead. When Lydia asked her why she wasn't coming, Sofia said that she would make a start on mending Mr Temba's shirts.

Whether or not to go to church was always a tricky question.

Sofia was not at all sure that she still believed in a good god of any kind. Not after Maria had died, and she herself had lost her legs.

How could a god who was good allow such things to happen?

Actually, she wasn't sure that Lydia believed in God either. But she did like singing, and enjoyed the sense of community in the packed church and gossiping afterwards with the other women.

Sofia had no idea what Rosa believed. Even though they shared so many secrets, they had never spoken about God together.

Sofia put on a red dress with a skirt that reached all the way down to her feet.

Then she closed the door behind her and started walking along a road that led away from the village. Soon the dusty road narrowed down to a track winding its way through tall grass. She kept a careful watch on the ground as she walked because there were plenty of poisonous snakes about.

Now and then she met people coming along the same path. Even though they didn't know her, they all greeted her and she greeted them back. The track was leading down the bank of a creek no more than a couple of metres wide. Later the creek joined the big river near Boane. There used to be crocodiles in this small creek, but now they had all migrated to the larger river.

When Sofia reached the water's edge, she felt hot and sweaty. She bent forward, leaning heavily on her crutches, and used one hand to scoop up some water.

She felt a little like a giraffe: stiff straight legs, bottom up in the air and one long arm stretched out, straining to reach the water.

She splashed some water on her forehead. Then she started walking again.

After walking another few hundred metres along the creek, she climbed the side of a small hill. When she got to the top she sat down.

This was Lion's Hill.

An old man had told her about it. Sofia had met him down by the river one day. He had spoken about the time when lions still hunted in the neighbourhood. A very large male had been seen resting on the top of the hill. It was the largest lion anyone could remember ever having seen. Nobody dared to go near it. Ever since, the place had been known as Lion's Hill.

Sofia had walked to Lion's Hill for the first time during the year after the terrible accident, when Maria had been killed and her own legs had been torn off. It was just after her return home from hospital. Her whole body ached and walking had been very difficult.

One day when she had been feeling sadder than usual, she had dragged herself down to the river bank to have some time on her own. That was when she discovered the hill.

Since then she always thought of Lion's Hill as a place

for sadness. She had even named it in her head: Sadness Place. She had never told anyone about it, of course. Least of all Rosa. It seemed such a childish thing. She still needed to be childish once in a while, but didn't want anyone to know.

But today she didn't feel sad at all. The dream from last night was still vivid in her mind and body.

Sitting on the top of the hill where the lion had been resting, she could see far away into the heat haze. In the distance, at the border to Swaziland, wave after wave of tall mountains rose into the sky.

The mountains had become one of the goals she longed to reach—to set out travelling one day, cross the high passes and find out what was on the other side. Would she really do it?

Today, Sofia just wanted to be alone on the hill. She needed to think about what had happened in the night. Well, anyway, in her dream about the boy.

In daylight, under the hot sun, the night seemed an alien place. There, a blue world was lit by the moon, blue sand had been trickling between her fingers and swells of seawater had been moving inside her. In that place, she had been together with the boy and had felt his body against her own.

It was a dream and not reality. Nothing had actually

happened. Yet the dream had reminded her of something that was real enough: her time had come now. She was fifteen years old and childhood was behind her. She was truly longing for a boy to call her own, who was there for her and her alone.

Sofia often despaired.

At times it seemed impossible that anyone should actually care for her like that. She, who had no legs and would never run or dance.

It was true that she might have other things to offer. She was going to school and knew how to read and write. Maybe she would become a teacher. That is, if she failed to train in medicine, for what she wanted most of all was to be a doctor.

Being a woman who was interesting to men was not just a matter of your face and body. With a good job, a house and a salary of her own, she would not lack boys and men pursuing her. Rosa and Lydia both kept telling her this, and even her teacher agreed that it was so.

She had to follow up so many lines of thought. Here on Lion's Hill, she would start with the most important ones, which had to do with becoming a woman—neither a child nor an almost-adult, but truly grown up. She felt sure that this was a turning point in her life. This was an event that happened once in a lifetime, like being born and dying.

She was lying back in the grass, looking up at the sky.

The sun was hot and she closed her eyes. Inside her head she was observing herself as she had been a few years ago. This was how she always saw Maria. Her sister could not grow older because she was dead. But now Sofia was watching her younger self walking away along the path. She waved goodbye to the little girl as she vanished round a bend.

She sat up. She was an adult now, and even though it had only been a dream, she knew what it was like to be with a man.

Then suddenly Maria seemed to be walking towards her along the path.

She was wearing her white dress as usual, but she was not alone. Sofia was walking next to her. They both looked just the way they had that morning when they were walking towards the explosion that was to tear them to pieces.

Sofia's eyes filled with tears.

What she had just experienced was denied to Maria, who would never sense the changes that came with growing up. The tears formed a mist over her eyes.

Then she shook her head. I mustn't cry, she told herself. Not today, anyway. Besides, what do I know? It may well be that the dead grow up—Maria, too.

Before leaving the hut, Sofia had hidden two things inside her dress—a grey notepad and a pencil. Her idea was to keep some kind of diary.

She had been planning for a long time to start writing down her thoughts. She would write only for herself, and maybe not every day. Rosa was sure to be curious, but she hadn't stayed on at school long enough to learn to read. Lydia usually left Sofia's things alone.

Now the time to start had arrived. She had saved the money she earned mending a pair of Mr Temba's trousers and bought the notepad at the marketplace next to her school. The pencil she had found on the road to school one day.

She found a comfortable position to sit and opened the pad.

The first page was blank and waiting for her. What would she begin with? It had to be what was most important to her just now: Moonboy. Then she would write about her dream. After that, about what was happening to her here at the top of Lion's Hill, as she was becoming aware of being a woman and of having left childhood behind.

She started writing down her thoughts, using few words and clear lettering. If she was unsure about how to spell a word, she left it out.

How did that poem in her dream go?

Love is blue.

She wrote it down. As she turned the first page, now filled with writing, she felt sure that sooner or later, the whole book would be full. It was slow and might take years. Maybe she would be an old woman before she turned the last page, but never mind. What mattered was that she had started.

She stayed on the hill all day.

The sun was setting when she finally got ready to walk back home. She realised that she had gone without food and was hungry, and that Mr Temba's shirts were waiting for her.

Still, that was all right. It had been a good day.

She wondered if becoming a woman would show somehow. Would anyone notice that she was not a child any more?

Walking into their yard, she stopped in amazement.

Their cooking pot, which had been stolen the night before, was standing by the fire.

ELEVEN

Lydia was very upset. She was shaking with anger.

'We're all just as poor, but still people keep stealing from each other,' she exclaimed.

Then she told Sofia what had happened.

When Lydia, Rosa and the boys came out of the church, they had taken a different way back. The idea was to pass by Mrs Chambule's place, because Lydia was keen to see her. Mrs Chambule had not been working in the fields for several days. Had she fallen ill? Was there anything Lydia could do to help? They had learnt that although Mrs Chambule was well, she had had to stay at home with a sick child. One of her many children had an attack of malarial fever.

They had been walking back home after visiting Mrs Chambule, when Lydia suddenly spotted her iron cooking pot in a front yard. It was standing in the grass outside a miserable-looking hut. She thought it might be her pot, because one of its three legs had a bit missing.

Lydia had told Rosa to wait in the road and keep an eye on Alfredo and Faustino. Then she crossed the yard and spoke to the people: two men, one woman and several children. Where had the cooking pot come from? The answers she was given were evasive. Coming closer, she recognised a scratch inside the pot. The whole situation made her very angry and she told them that she would take the pot back, because it was hers and had been stolen from her.

The men had tried to argue, but Lydia was determined. If they did not hand back the pot, she threatened to ask the village elder to come and order them to. The row grew as other people came along and joined in the excitement.

Lydia stood her ground. She finally got her pot back after declaring that she would walk all the way to Boane and complain to the police.

Telling this story made Lydia so upset she broke out in a sweat. Not only was she still angry, but also very sad. Lydia's forehead became wrinkled when she was upset. Anger gave her two deep furrows from the hairline to her nose, and sadness created little wrinkles all over. Right now, her forehead showed both patterns.

'Of course, I could see that they were as poor as we are,' she said. 'Maybe even worse off. The children looked scared and hungry, and their clothes were in tatters. But never mind that, it just won't do to steal from other poor people. That doesn't help anyone.'

Sofia memorised what Lydia had said. She would write it down in her diary.

They ate early that evening. Sunday night was Lydia's time to go visiting her sister Alicia, who lived at the far end of the village. Sofia and Rosa often went with her, but not tonight. Lydia set out, taking only Alfredo and Faustino.

Rosa and Sofia were alone. Rosa noticed Sofia closing her notepad and putting her pencil down.

'What are you writing?' Rosa asked.

'Just something for myself.'

'Come on. I asked you what it is.'

'It's private.'

'But we share all our secrets.'

'No, we don't. You don't tell me everything.'

It was a quiet, still night.

While she talked, Rosa had been looking at herself in their piece of mirror-glass. Sofia thought Rosa seemed like her usual self. The tiredness had gone.

'Hey, let's go out,' Rosa said suddenly.

'Where to?'

'Hassan's shop.'

Sofia felt embarrassed. She had always hoped that Rosa would ask her along, but it scared her, too. She both did and did not want to go.

'I've got to go to school tomorrow,' she said hesitantly. 'I should go to bed early.'

'We won't be late.'

'I don't know. You'd better go on your own.'

Rosa put the mirror back on the wall.

'You must come,' she said decisively. 'You've got to meet some new people. Really, you only talk to us and your mates at school.'

Sofia still didn't feel happy about it.

'Who'll be there?' she asked.

'Oh, you never know. All kinds of people. You should know some of them at least, but there may be a lot of new ones.'

Rosa almost pushed Sofia in front of her to the corner where her clothes were. Then she started to pick over Sofia's few things.

'Put this one on,' she said. It was a blue blouse.

Sofia obeyed. She refused to put on her other skirt, though. It was too short, she felt, because it did not quite reach down to the top of her shoes.

Rosa looked her over critically.

'You're really pretty,' she said. 'But it shows that you don't think so yourself.'

'*You* are pretty,' Sofia said. 'I'm fat and not at all good-looking. Besides I don't have normal legs.'

'You're alive,' Rosa said, sounding almost irritated. 'Maria isn't. Come on, let's go.'

It was getting darker now.

Rosa was walking so quickly that Sofia could hardly keep up. The closer they came to Hassan's shop, the more nervous she felt. She stopped.

'I'm going back home,' she said. 'I won't come.'

'Don't be silly. What's supposed to be so frightening? Just tell me.'

Sofia wasn't frightened of anything dangerous. What she feared was that nobody would notice her, or not care whether she was there or not.

'Come on now,' Rosa said. 'Hassan might have some new magazines.'

'It's Sunday, maybe the shop's closed,' Sofia said. She hoped that it would be closed so that they would have to go back home again.

'Hassan's shop is always open,' Rosa replied. 'Don't fuss.'

Hassan was sitting on a tall stool, reading an old, dog-eared newspaper. A paraffin lamp on the counter cast a circle of light in the room. He was a small man with a short, bluntly-cut beard. He looked up when Rosa and Sofia came in and narrowed his eyes.

'Rosa,' he said, sounding almost unhappy. 'I've been wondering what had happened to you. I was beginning to think that I would never see you again.'

This surprised Sofia. So Hassan knew Rosa and had actually missed her? Did he know everyone who came to his shop? All the other young people, too, who came to look at his magazines and never bought anything?

'This is my sister,' Rosa said, dragging Sofia into the light. Hassan's eyes met Sofia's. Then his glance travelled over her, stopping briefly at her crutches and then her long skirt. He shook his head and sighed.

'I know,' he said. 'Everyone knows about Sofia. She's the one who survived.'

Hassan slid off his stool and went to look for something in the shadows behind the counter. He came back with a bar of chocolate, which he gave Sofia. She was so confused at being the centre of attention that she forgot to thank him.

The one who survived.

Was that who she was? Her cheeks felt hot. She knew she was blushing and backed out of the lamplight.

'Have you got any new magazines?' Rosa asked.

Hassan sighed again.

'I'm sorry, no,' he said. 'Maybe next week, with any luck.'

Then he pushed his spectacles into place and started reading again.

Rosa pulled Sofia outside.

It was really dark by now, but the night was lit by the flames of a big fire. It had been built on the ground, close to the shop. Sofia glimpsed people moving about in the shadows. Someone laughed, someone else was singing.

Rosa started talking to a boy she knew. He was wearing a cap the wrong way round. After a while, Rosa forgot about Sofia and disappeared into the crowd.

Sofia became furious.

This was turning out exactly as she had feared. No one was taking any notice of her. She simply was not seen by anyone and so she stayed an outsider. Not even Rosa, her own sister, had any time for her.

A boy close to the fire started to play the drums and Rosa danced to the beat. Soon others were dancing, too. Sofia walked off to stand away from the group.

That Rosa! Why had she insisted? Rosa didn't care one bit about her sister, really.

Hassan came out of the shop and noticed Sofia.

'It's not necessary to go dancing,' he said. 'Look at me! I've got legs but still don't dance.'

Sofia knew he was trying to cheer her up, but it just

made her feel even worse. She did not want to be comforted. By now, she just wanted to be somewhere else. And, more than anything, she wanted to have normal legs.

Hassan stood there for a while, contemplating his pipe. It had gone out. He sighed once more and went back inside the shop.

Sofia made up her mind quickly. She backed away cautiously until she was completely swallowed up by the darkness, and then walked off.

It would serve Rosa right if she had to go looking for her and worry almost as much as Sofia had been worrying about her after she dropped the hoe. Tit for tat.

After walking for a long while, Sofia stopped.

It was hard to work out where she was in the dark landscape. She felt drops of rain against her face. She decided on what she thought was the right direction, and set out again. She saw fires fading around her as she walked. The village was getting ready to rest for the night.

More and more raindrops fell on her face. She walked as quickly as she could, but even so she was wet through when she arrived home.

Lydia was standing in the doorway.

'Where's Rosa?' she asked.

'At Hassan's shop.'

'Have you been there, too?'

Sofia did not bother to answer. She went into the other room and pulled the curtain across the door. Lydia left her in peace.

Sofia took off her wet clothes and then her legs, and crawled into bed. It had been a long day. She wasn't angry with Rosa any more. She had meant well, surely.

Sofia pulled the cover up to her chin and closed her eyes. She went to sleep, wondering if she'd have to wait until the next full moon before the boy in the road came back.

TWELVE

෨෧

Another month went by. The moon was growing full again.

The air was hotter and more humid than before. The rainy season was drawing closer. There had been a few heavy downpours already. Often, Sofia woke in the middle of the night, soaked in sweat.

It didn't seem to matter any more to Sofia that the boy had not come back. Her boy, who had been standing there once in the blue light of the moon.

So, maybe he had just come to her in a dream—the dream that had made her a woman.

But nothing mattered any more, not even that, because Rosa had dropped the hoe again.

This time, she had been too weak to pick it up.

It had happened a few days after the day that had ended with Sofia and Rosa going to Hassan's shop.

By the time Rosa came back, Sofia had already fallen asleep. The following day, they both avoided talking about going to the shop. Sofia saw guilt written all over Rosa's face, and understood why. Rosa had abandoned Sofia and left her to face the rest of the evening alone, without giving her a second thought.

Rosa had fallen ill this time in the same way as before. She had complained of tiredness, and dropped the hoe when she set out to clear the weeds from among the growing corn.

Sofia had not seen this for herself, because she had been to school that day. Rosa told her later how she felt. She had no appetite, and waves of fever kept coming and going.

Sofia had felt the cold lump form in her stomach again. It grew colder and heavier as the days went by and Rosa failed to recover. Lydia was very worried, too.

Rosa just kept saying that she would get better soon. All she needed was a little more rest.

The days passed and became weeks. Soon the full moon would be back in the sky, but Rosa was still unwell.

It was obvious to Sofia that Rosa had lost a lot of weight. Her stomach was upset and she had to go outside several times each night. Sofia would wake and lie in bed waiting for Rosa to come back. She never got an answer when she asked Rosa how she felt. Rosa would just curl up on her mat again and go to sleep. Even when she slept, her breathing sounded as if she had been running hard and every breath was an effort.

Sofia attended school each weekday between the two full moons, but she found it hard to concentrate on the work. One day, Miss Adelina told her to stay behind.

'What's the matter, Sofia?' she asked. 'You're usually so alert, but for the last few weeks it's been easy to see that you often don't pay attention to the lessons.'

'I'm sorry. Rosa is ill,' Sofia replied.

'Who's Rosa?'

'My sister.'

'Is it a serious illness?'

'I don't know.'

Miss Adelina asked no more questions, because she believed the explanation and understood why Sofia seemed absentminded at times.

During the weeks that passed, Sofia mended most of Mr Temba's shirts. Somehow, she never got round to the blue one though. Like a bad conscience, it was hidden at the bottom of her pile of sewing.

Now and then she would pull it out and look at it. Each time she did, mending it so that Mr Temba would not notice the strip cut out of the back seemed just as impossible.

One afternoon, Mr Temba turned up outside their hut. As usual, he was wearing his hat. Also, he carried an umbrella, because the rainy season was so close. He wouldn't get very wet if he hurried home from their place, Sofia thought. Clearly he didn't want to risk it anyway.

Mr Temba had come to ask about his blue shirt. Sofia felt a sharp cramp somewhere inside.

'It's one of my favourite shirts,' Mr Temba said. Then he bowed to her and went on his way.

Sofia knew exactly what he meant. He wanted his shirt back soon, say, in two or, at most, three days time.

That evening, before Sofia had a chance to start on the blue shirt, they came to a joint decision: Rosa must go to the doctor. She didn't want to and argued against it, but Lydia and Sofia refused to listen to her. By then Rosa had been poorly for more than a month.

The health centre was near the school, so they agreed that Sofia would stay on after school and wait for Rosa. Sofia finished school at half past twelve, so there would be plenty of time to see the doctor. He came to their centre only two days a week, on Tuesdays and Thursdays. The following day was a Thursday.

'I don't want to go. It's unnecessary,' Rosa said.

Please dear God, Sofia thought. I've tried so hard not to believe that there's an illness inside Rosa. I can't keep the possibility that it's there out of my mind any longer.

I don't want to think about it, I don't want to know. But I must.

That night, Sofia could not go to sleep.

The full moon shone in the sky. She tried to think about the boy in the road, but it didn't work and the dream did not come back. Maybe it was because Rosa was sleeping on the floor next to her. Rosa's presence had nothing to do with dreams. She was lying there for real, breathing with short, strained breaths, and twisting and turning in her sleep.

The next day was overcast.

In the distance, Sofia saw constant flashes of lightning illuminating the heavy clouds over the Swaziland mountain range. The storm was drawing nearer, but the rumble and crack of thunder was not yet audible.

Rosa came walking along the road to the school.

She was moving slowly, almost unwillingly. Sofia's stomach seemed to grow colder and she slapped it irritably. If only she could stop worrying.

She went to meet Rosa. When she came close, she realised that Rosa was afraid. It was written all over her face. Her eyes were flickering anxiously, but coming back again and again to Sofia's face to search for a sign that everything was all right. Sofia looked down. She could not bear looking her sister in the eye.

Why did everything seem so hard?

The truth is hard. Only the truth would do, but they didn't yet know what it was.

Perhaps it would be what Rosa wanted and hoped for. Maybe she just needed rest to get better.

Rosa was sweating and she said that her stomach hurt.

It was not yet one o'clock. That morning, Sofia had gone to the health centre and spoken to the doctor about Rosa. He had noted her name and asked Sofia what seemed to be wrong with her sister. Sofia told him exactly what she had observed: Rosa was too tired to work or do anything energetic, and was losing weight and suffering from bouts of fever and an almost constantly upset stomach.

The doctor nodded. He did not comment at all. Sofia tried to read his face, but there were no words to be found.

The two sisters sat down in the shade of an old, burnt-out bus lying at the roadside—a reminder of the war. Sofia thought of the bandits who had murdered her father.

The thunder was rolling in the distance.

'We'll get wet on the way home,' Rosa said.

Then they sat in silence.

While they waited, some schoolboys were playing football nearby and shouting to each other. Sofia could not take her eyes away from the health centre. The doctor was in there, ready to examine Rosa. He would tell them the truth.

'We'd better go now,' Sofia said, and heaved herself up with the help of her crutches.

Rosa did not move. Sofia waited.

'We'd better go,' she said again. 'It's one o'clock and the doctor is waiting for you.'

They walked into the dark waiting room, where a nurse was sitting doing some paperwork and trying to swat an irritating fly.

'Dr Nkeka is with a patient just now,' she said. 'He won't be long. She's only pregnant.'

When the pregnant woman came out, they saw that she had a huge stomach and must be close to term. It wouldn't be long before she gave birth.

Birth and death, Sofia thought. She imagined herself wearing a white coat and sitting at the desk in the inner room. Rosa would be someone else, not her sister at all.

Rosa got up. 'Please come with me,' she whispered.

But the nurse heard her.

'Only the patient,' she said sternly.

Rosa disappeared through the door and it shut behind her.

Sofia waited. She tried to guess what was going on in that room. The nurse yawned and kept swatting at the stubborn fly. The room was very hot. The storm was coming closer.

Sofia started when the door suddenly opened and Dr Nkeka came out. He was a young man, but his hair was already turning grey. He nodded to Sofia and asked the nurse to step inside. If only I had been the fly, Sofia thought, then I could have kept buzzing around the nurse and listened to what the doctor would say.

The thunder was almost overhead. An old man came into the room. He was leaning heavily on his stick. When he asked for the doctor, Sofia pretended that she was the nurse. 'The doctor is busy with a patient,' she told him.

The man was hard of hearing.

'The doctor is busy,' she shouted.

The man sat down to wait. She could hear the rattling in his lungs when he coughed.

The door opened and the nurse came out first. Then Rosa. The nurse looked displeased when she noticed the old man. As the girls set out to walk home from the health centre, Sofia hoped that they wouldn't get caught in the rain.

She noticed a prick mark at Rosa's inner elbow.

'What did the doctor say?' she asked.

'He wanted the nurse to take a blood sample. I'm supposed to come back for the result on Tuesday.'

'Didn't he tell you anything else?'

'He wanted to know how I was, but he didn't tell me anything.'

'Nothing at all?'

'Only about the sample and going back to see him on Tuesday.'

Sofia had no idea what this might mean. Why had Dr Nkeka been so uncommunicative? There must have been a reason for the blood sample.

It started to rain and they walked as quickly as they could.

Next Tuesday they would know what was wrong with Rosa.

THIRTEEN

⊚∞

The days dragged by.

Usually, Sofia thought that four days passed quite quickly. She had learnt patience during the long months in hospital, but this waiting was different. Time moved at a snail's pace. Not that she really wanted next Tuesday to come, anyway.

For as long as Rosa's test result was not known, no one could say for sure that she was seriously ill. Only Dr Nkeka's sample could decide that.

They had been wet through when they arrived home after visiting the health centre. It had rained heavily for most of the way.

Lydia asked at once what had happened. Because the doctor had said nothing, except to come back later, Lydia believed that whatever it was couldn't have been so bad. She was like that. She often worried about things, but could not bear having to plan for possible future problems. Sofia found it hard to work out what Rosa thought. In many ways Rosa was like Lydia. She became anxious and upset easily, but forgot just as easily.

The spell of bad weather lasted all weekend. It poured with rain and the yard looked like a swamp.

Lydia worried that the *machamba* would flood. On Sunday morning she set out to walk all the way there, in spite of the heavy rain. She wanted to see for herself if the *machamba* was under water.

It didn't help much. She was a little happier, because the water level had not yet risen enough for the vegetables and corn to rot, but on the other hand, it was worrying to think that the rain might continue.

While it rained, Sofia mended Mr Temba's blue shirt. She had thought hard about it before she started. Now she really had to think of a cunning way to disguise where the shirt had a strip of material cut out from the back. In the end, the mend looked better than she dared to hope. Rosa looked over the finished shirt and couldn't understand what the fuss was about. The shirt looked fine. Lydia, too, didn't notice anything wrong. Sofia began to hope that she might get away with it. No one would know what she'd been up to during that night of the full moon.

She sometimes thought of Moonboy before going to sleep, but it was becoming harder to imagine his face. Her dreams were happening more and more in the dark.

During those days she often talked with Maria.

She had told Maria about Rosa. Now she told her about the visit to the health centre, and about the doctor ordering a blood sample. All the time, Maria looked at her but didn't say anything. Sofia wondered if maybe the dead know the future. The living don't know, not even what will happen the next day, and so they have to keep worrying.

By Monday morning, the clouds started to lift at last. The yard was still waterlogged, but the ground had dried quickly after the sun had come out.

Rosa went outside to check on the road. If it was too muddy, Sofia couldn't move on her crutches and her stiff legs would get stuck. Miss Adelina knew that on some days, when it had been raining heavily, Sofia would not be in school.

When Rosa came back, she was shaking her head. It was far too muddy. Sofia would get stuck.

Sofia sat down on the edge of her bed and took her school books out of her rucksack. She was determined to make up for not going to school by studying at home instead.

She could see Rosa through the doorway to the other room, which was lit by sunlight coming through the open outside door. She was looking at herself in the mirror.

Sofia kept an eye on her for a while. It seemed impossible that Rosa should be suffering from that disease.

116

She pushed her worries away. She must try to become like Lydia, who never worried in advance.

Rosa called out to her.

'Mr Temba's coming!'

Sofia jumped. The book fell off her lap. This was it.

Mr Temba stepped in through the open door and bowed to Rosa.

'The rains seem to have gone away for now,' he said politely.

At once, it came into Sofia's mind how much she liked the way Mr Temba spoke, thoughtfully and pleasantly. He seemed fond of the words he used and they passed his lips in an orderly, gentle flow. He was never hurried and chose his words with care.

There were those who became impatient with him—Lydia for one. She said he was a slowcoach. She talked so fast herself that the words came rushing out.

Sofia brought the shirt out for Mr Temba, who bowed.

'I noticed that you didn't go to school today, Sofia,' he said. 'I hope I've not disturbed you by coming to collect my blue shirt.'

Sofia shook her head and handed him the shirt.

Mr Temba shook it out, held it up and turned it over. Sofia had palpitations. Would he discover what she had done? He looked gravely at her. He's noticed, she thought. Now he'll never ask me to mend his clothes

117

again. The whole village will get to know that Sofia can't be trusted. She destroys your clothes, so don't give her any mending to do.

Mr Temba's face still looked serious. By now she was too scared to look away.

'You've mended it beautifully', he said.

She could hardly believe her ears. He sounded perfectly sincere. A moment later he produced some notes from his pocket and handed them to her.

'I plan to go visiting a very significant person tonight,' he said. 'My intention is to wear this shirt.' Then Mr Temba bowed in farewell and left.

Rosa giggled.

'Mr Temba is going to be with one of his women tonight and Mrs Mukulela will be furious. She's so difficult. She gets angry when other women make love to him and just as angry when he tries to get her to do it.'

Sofia looked after Mr Temba as he picked his way between the muddy patches in their yard. It was true that he made love with lots of different women. Maybe he, too, would catch the dangerous disease. Just like Rosa, he might have it already, without it showing.

Sofia returned to her school books, but couldn't concentrate. Her thoughts kept circling around one image that had stuck in her mind: Rosa's face when she came through the door after seeing Dr Nkeka.

That night, Sofia had a strange dream.

She had gone across to Mr Temba's place to hand over a pair of trousers she had mended. When she knocked, a strange man opened the door. Sofia got the feeling she had seen him somewhere, though. Then she realised that the man was her father. He was still young.

Her father asked her to step inside. When he closed the door behind her, she saw that the room had no walls. Instead they were on a beach by the sea, where the waves were beating against the sand.

She followed her father down to the water's edge. The waves tumbled seashells along in the sand. He pointed to an island that could just be glimpsed through the heat haze.

'That's where I live,' he said. 'I just wanted you to know.'

After telling her this, her father walked into the sea, still wearing his clothes. When the water reached up to his chest, he turned, waved to her and started to swim away.

Sofia stayed there, watching his head until it disappeared among the waves. She felt filled with a mysterious joy. Then she slowly walked back to Mr Temba's house, went through the door and stepped straight back into the ordinary world.

When she woke from her dream, Mrs Mukulela's rooster was crowing. Rosa was still asleep.

Sofia stayed in bed, thinking about her dream. Had it told her anything? Messages in dreams always seemed to be riddles. She tried to decode the meaning of the dream, but got nowhere. Maybe her father had simply wanted to make contact with her?

Sofia's reached out her hand and stroked Rosa's hair lightly with her fingertips.

The night before, Sofia had braided her hair. It had taken hours to do, but had turned out very well. Rosa had asked for a pattern of stars to cover her scalp. She wanted to look good when she saw Dr Nkeka again.

While she was lying back with her head on Sofia's lap, getting her new hair-do, Rosa had suddenly asked a question.

'Do you think I'm seriously ill?'

'Not at all,' Sofia had replied.

But she had answered too rapidly and too reassuringly. Sofia felt that she couldn't say what she really thought: Rosa was suffering from that dreadful disease that sneaked into people's lives and in the end, killed them.

Sofia could not say this. She didn't dare.

At one o'clock on Tuesday, Sofia was waiting for Rosa again outside the health centre.

That day, Miss Adelina had noticed that Sofia didn't pay much attention to the lessons. In spite of that, the teacher didn't say anything. She understood why Sofia was so distracted.

The last storm clouds had drifted away and the sun was shining in a cloudless sky. Sofia was waiting in the shade of a tree near where the boys were playing football. She watched them. Their feet were moving so quickly, running and leaping and then hitting the ground when they landed after a jump. She tried to imagine having real legs and feet, but failed.

Rosa came walking along the road.

She reached Sofia, stopped and wiped the sweat from her forehead. Sofia looked over the braids from the night before. She was really pleased with the result.

They went into the health centre together. The nurse was sitting there with her flyswat at the ready. She nodded at the door.

'Step inside,' she said. 'He's free now.'

The door closed behind Rosa.

Sofia sat down on a sofa with a worn plastic cover. Her heart was beating so hard it was difficult to breathe. There was not a single thought in her head.

She soon lost any idea of how long she'd been sitting there. Finally the door opened.

Rosa came out.

FOURTEEN

∾

Late that evening, after nightfall, Sofia lit her candle and started writing in her notepad, sitting up in bed. Rosa was already asleep.

I do not know what I feel. Maybe tired, sad and afraid. Or afraid, tired and sad. Or whichever way round. In any case, it's bad news. For as long as I didn't know, there was a cold lump in my stomach. Now, the chill has spread right through my body. My legs feel cold too, even though they are not there. Today Dr Nkeka told Rosa that she has caught a disease called AIDS. He explained that it is a serious illness, but gave her some hope of living for a long time if she looks after herself. She must eat lots of vegetables, think happy thoughts and carry on leading her life the way she always has, from first thing in the morning until late at night. I write this at night. The clouds are thick and cover the moon. I feel lonely. I don't

know what is the worst—being so tired or so afraid or
so terribly sad.

Sofia put her writing things away and blew out the candle. The night air was stuffy. She heard the rumble of thunder from very far away, maybe even from the other side of the Swaziland border.

Sofia kept staring wide-eyed into the darkness.

Her thoughts would not stop going back to the moment when Rosa first stepped out of Dr Nkeka's room. Rosa's face had seemed to express relief, but that was a mistake.

Rosa's stiff movements gave away how scared she was. Before she could say anything, Dr Nkeka came out. In spite of smiling, he looked really distressed.

'I'm very, very sorry,' he said. 'Your sister is seriously ill. You've got to help each other to cope. That's all I can advise.'

They left the health centre. Tears were streaming down Rosa's face. She wept silently, in terror.

Sofia stopped, let her crutches fall and hugged her sister. Now Rosa seemed to be a small child. Gone was the beautiful, self-assured and careless young woman who had been dancing outside Hassan's shop.

'I don't want to die,' she whispered. 'Not die. Not now, not yet.'

'You won't die,' Sofia told her. 'No one is going to die. Least of all you.'

After a while, they started walking again. In bursts, as if it was almost unbearable to speak, Rosa told Sofia what Dr Nkeka had said.

He had asked her to sit down. For a while he just looked at her and moved things about on his desk, as if he did not want to start speaking. Then he told her the truth, in plain language.

'Your blood sample shows that you have caught an infection. It's a virus called HIV. Do you know what this means? Have you ever heard of the virus?'

Rosa had just shaken her head.

'The virus is in your blood. Sooner or later it will cause you to develop a disease called AIDS. You must have heard of AIDS?'

Rosa shook her head again. Actually, she had heard of AIDS, because Sofia had been telling her about it. At the time, she had felt that not knowing somehow made her less vulnerable.

Dr Nkeka explained that it was almost impossible to cure AIDS. The disease grew worse slowly, step by step. At present, Rosa was somewhere mid-way between catching the infection and developing full-blown AIDS. Rosa felt confused about what this meant exactly.

Then the doctor had started asking her really difficult questions of a kind no one had ever asked her before.

When was the last time she had made love with some-one? How many boys had she been with? At first, Rosa felt like running away to avoid having to answer his questions. He had insisted that it was important for him to know, and in the end she told him. She had made love with four different boys. Not more than that. But she didn't know if any one of them had been ill.

As he went on questioning her, she felt better about answering, because he didn't seem angry with her and didn't scold her for anything.

He was particularly interested in Steven from South Africa. He had been twenty-five years old.

He was the one Rosa had loved best. Sofia had met him. Then, suddenly, he had gone back to South Africa and they never heard from him again. Dr Nkeka said that in Rosa's case, Steven was the most likely source of infection.

Then came the most difficult question of all. Had the boys used any protection when they made love? Rosa had just shaken her head. She had only the vaguest idea of what he was talking about.

Dr Nkeka asked her to tell the boys she had slept with to come along to the health centre. Their blood samples must be tested, too, because otherwise they wouldn't know if they were carriers of the virus. It was important to avoid having them infect anybody else.

Then he told her what she had to do for herself.

Above all, she was to live as usual. She should eat and sleep well, and try not to worry all the time. He wanted her to come to see him every month. If she became worse, or if her upset stomach and diarrhoea didn't get better, she must come to ask his advice as soon as possible.

Then he gave her some medicines and explained how she should take them. They would not make her well, he told her, but might help her feel better.

Somewhere along the road, Rosa had suddenly stopped.

'Does it have to mean death to be in love with some-one?' she asked. 'And if it does, what's the point of living?'

Sofia had no answers. They walked on in silence.

When they passed Hassan's shop, Rosa turned her head away. Sofia knew that she had met Steven for the first time outside the shop.

When they were very nearly home, Rosa stopped and looked pleadingly at Sofia.

'I don't want to tell Lydia today,' she said. 'Please, let's not. I can't bear it. Couldn't it wait till tomorrow?'

'Of course it can wait,' Sofia replied. 'But you know

that Lydia will be worrying and wondering. We've got to say something.'

'Maybe we could tell her that the results from the blood sample aren't known yet?'

'No, she won't believe that,' Sofia said. 'Dr Nkeka is such a good, reliable doctor. If he says something will be ready on a certain day, then it will be. Everybody knows that.'

Sofia noticed that Rosa was about to start crying again. She seemed close to breaking down all the time.

'We'll tell her that there's something wrong with your stomach,' Sofia said. 'And that's why you've got to go back to see the doctor again.'

Rosa looked at her gratefully.

They went into their yard.

Lydia was there, waiting for them. She had obviously been too worried to stay at the *machamba* and left earlier than usual. She looked carefully at Rosa.

'What did the doctor say?'

'I've got a sore stomach.'

'That's not news to us. Didn't he tell you what it was? And if it's serious?'

'Rosa must go back and see him again,' Sofia said. 'And he said she mustn't talk too much, just rest and take her medicines.'

Lydia did not ask any more questions.

Rosa went inside and lay down on Sofia's bed. She curled up with her knees drawn up to her chin, like a baby in the womb, to protect herself against panic.

Sofia's heart ached when she looked at her sister. It was still unreal to her that Rosa would die soon. Not tomorrow, not next week, but not a long time from now and anyway, far too early. Despair grew inside her, hot like a fever. The cold lump in her stomach had turned to embers that glowed and burnt her.

Quietly she sat down on the edge of the bed. She put her hand on Rosa's head.

'I don't want to die,' Rosa whispered.

'Of course you won't,' Sofia said. 'Of course you won't die.'

Rosa didn't want anything to eat.

'I'll go out and talk to Lydia,' Sofia said. 'She'll just start worrying again if I don't.'

Rosa did not answer. She was curled up into herself.

Sofia went out into the yard. It was getting darker.

Sofia looked at Lydia. Now she would lose another child.

She did not know it yet.

Sofia felt alone, left on her own inside a huge lonely space.

She had been losing people all her life. First the

bandits had killed her father. He had returned to her in a dream to talk to her and point out his island home. But that was not enough, because she needed him alive. He should have been there at the fire, next to Lydia.

Then she lost Maria.

She came back, too, but only for a short time after waking at dawn, when dreams were still lingering.

Walking back from the health centre, Sofia had tried to remember everything Deolinda had told her from her hospital bed. How long could one live with the disease? Deolinda had heard that in other countries, there were people with plenty of money who could buy expensive medicines. These medicines, and having the best doctors and a really good life, meant that they could live for as long as practically anybody else.

That certainly was not true for Rosa. Sofia thought of how much she hated the poverty of their lives. She recalled what she had heard about the rich. They had as much money as they could use and then some. They drove past poor people in big smart cars with darkened windows.

Sofia had no idea how long Rosa had to live. She decided to fight for her and protect her sister for as long as she could.

Rosa was not to die. She must live.

They ate their supper by the fire.

Lydia asked only once if Sofia could tell her any more about what was wrong with Rosa. Sofia shook her head. It was very difficult to lie to Lydia. Sofia had promised not to tell for now, but Lydia would know soon enough.

Tomorrow she would be told what Dr Nkeka had said. Already, Sofia agonised about how Lydia would react.

They went to bed early that night. When the house was silent, Sofia took out her diary. She wrote down what she thought and felt.

Beyond the words, awareness dawned of what was most important to her. What she was longing for.

It was to not be alone, now that Rosa was ill.

The boy in the road. If only he existed and could help her now. She had never needed him like this before.

FIFTEEN

~∞~

Next day was just as miserable as Sofia had feared. In the morning, the heavy clouds covered the sky. There was still no rain.

Sofia knew that Lydia was waiting. They could not keep it from her any more. She had been awake and moving about in the hut that night, enough to wake Sofia. This was not like her. Sofia understood that Lydia was worrying too much to sleep.

They must tell her now. Her dear Rosa had the terrible illness that everyone felt they could not even speak about.

Rosa began but did not manage to get the story together. Sofia had to take over.

They had just finished their morning meal. Lydia was getting ready to leave for her walk to the *machamba*. Then she learnt the truth. She was told what Dr Nkeka had said.

Lydia became still and quiet. Sofia tried to tell her

everything exactly as she herself knew it, but as gently as possible.

At one point, a thought fluttered through her head like an anxious bird. I'm far too young to explain these difficult subjects to my mother.

But there was no one else.

Rosa was far too frightened and confused. Sofia was the only one who could speak plainly about it and tell Lydia what had happened.

Lydia put down her hoe. In his bundle on her back, Faustino slept on. Alfredo was sitting a little apart and drawing in the sand. Sofia knew that he was taking in every word they said. She had never met anyone who could listen like Alfredo. He surely wouldn't change when he grew up, but always be someone who listened carefully and said little.

Lydia kept looking from Sofia to Rosa and back again.

'There must be some medicine that can cure this illness,' she said.

'No, there isn't,' Sofia replied. 'All you can do is try to live your life as usual.'

Suddenly Lydia attacked Rosa angrily.

'I told you, didn't I? You shouldn't go running after boys at night. Look what's happened! You should've listened to me!'

Rosa kept her eyes fixed on the ground. Sofia tried to

catch Lydia's attention and look stern. Being angry with Rosa helped nobody.

'I know what we must do,' Lydia said firmly. 'Visit a *curandiero*. We'll consult Mr Nombora. I've heard that he can cure this disease.'

Sofia knew who Mr Nombora was. He lived in one of the villages to the west of theirs.

Mr Nombora had created quite a lot of excitement when he put up this sign outside his house:

DOCTOR NOMBORA CAN CURE YOUR AIDS
& AT THE SAME TIME
HIS BROTHER CAN MEND YOUR BROKEN BICYCLE.

Sofia didn't quite know what to say.

During her long stay in hospital, she had chatted to many patients who had ended up there after visiting a *curandiero* for some time. They had turned to the *curandiero* for help with something that troubled them. Instead of getting better, they became so ill that they had to go into hospital.

Sofia was full of respect for the people who were *curandieros*. They also frightened her.

They knew magic, and could see things nobody else could. They could make people ill as well as curing the sick. It was dangerous to have a *curandiero* as your enemy.

At the same time, she doubted a lot of what was said about them. They had talked about *curandieros* in school and been told that they could not really carry out supernatural feats. So Sofia was doubtful about the idea, but Lydia really believed in the *curandiero's* skills as much as in Dr Nkeka's.

'We'll consult Mr Nombora,' Lydia said again. Then she looked at Sofia. 'Do you have any of the money from Mr Temba left? It will have to be used for paying Mr Nombora.'

Sofia hesitated. It wasn't the money that worried her, but the idea of taking Rosa to see Mr Nombora. After all, Dr Nkeka had said there was no cure.

'Maybe we should wait a little,' Sofia said uncertainly.

'Why wait?'

Sofia could not think of a good reason.

'I want to go to Mr Nombora,' Rosa said. 'I want to get better.'

Sofia realised that there was no point in arguing now.

If Lydia and Rosa agreed, it didn't matter what she said. Besides, there might be a chance that Mr Nombora would actually help Rosa. It was impossible to know for sure.

Still, Sofia feared that Rosa could get even worse. Mr Nombora might give her one of his little bottles of medicine. What they contained, no one ever knew.

They stopped talking.

Sofia suddenly felt sick. Worry and fear had built up inside her so much that it suddenly had to get out. She hurried over to a tree and vomited.

'Sofia, are you unwell, too?' Lydia asked anxiously.

'I'm fine,' Sofia said. 'There's nothing wrong.'

Still, she threw up several times that day. There were too many feelings hidden inside her. It took time to become free of them.

Rosa was weeding their little field. She was singing while she struck the hoe against the hard ground between the corn plants to rip out the weeds.

Sofia had stayed at home from school because she was sick such a lot. When she observed Rosa at work she thought that she was doing exactly the right things. She didn't give up. She worked, and sang while she worked. That's what Dr Nkeka had told her to do. *Live as usual.* For Rosa, life meant working and singing. Not lying curled up on the floor and crying.

Lydia had left to walk to the *machamba.*

Before she left, she told Sofia and Rosa what had happened that morning. It had been quite unexpected. She was giggling, as if she were as young as her daughters.

They all felt in need of a break from the heavy seriousness of Rosa's illness.

Lydia told them that she had seen Mr Temba come out of Mrs Mukulela's hut that morning.

Both Rosa and Sofia became interested at once. Had Mr Temba really managed to break down Mrs Mukulela's defences?

'Did he see you?' Rosa asked.

'I quickly turned my back,' Lydia replied. 'I can't wait to see what will happen next.'

'What did he look like?' Rosa went on.

Sofia thought that at least for the moment Rosa had pushed illness out of her mind.

'His shirt was unbuttoned,' giggled Lydia. 'He was wearing a blue shirt. I think it was the last one Sofia mended for him.'

'He said he was going visiting,' Sofia told them. 'But he didn't tell me it was Mrs Mukulela he was going to see.'

Just then, Mrs Mukulela came out into her yard.

Mr Temba was already sitting in the usual place outside his door, working at his baskets. Pretending not to take any notice, Lydia, Rosa and Sofia were watching him and listening hard. They heard the two of them exchange polite good mornings and remarks about the weather.

'Mr Temba is not making a fuss about the rooster,' Sofia said. 'And that's in spite of it making a really awful noise this morning.'

That made them all start giggling again. For a while, Sofia, too, had forgotten about Rosa's disease.

In the afternoon, Sofia spent some time in the hut cleaning the sewing machine. Rosa came in and sat down on the bed.

'Dr Nkeka told me I had to be careful. What do you think he meant?'

Sofia understood at once what Rosa was thinking. She realised that she could no longer sleep with a boy if she felt like it. Now they could be infected by her, just as she had become infected by someone, probably Steven. For their sakes, she must be careful.

Dr Nkeka had said something else as well. If Rosa made love with a boy, she must see to it that he wore a condom to protect them both.

Sofia was not sure Rosa even knew what he meant by 'a condom'. She reached for one of her plastic bags, which she used for things she wanted to keep. Several months ago, health care people from the capital city had come to the school as part of their travels round the country. They were telling everyone about the serious illness and ways to protect yourself against it. They brought condoms and explained how to use them, even though lots of people in the class were giggling. Everybody got a packet of condoms to take away. Many of Sofia's classmates larked about after school and blew the condoms up like balloons, but Sofia had kept her packet and put it in her rucksack.

Now she took one condom out of the packet and tried to explain it to Rosa. Sofia noticed how embarrassed Rosa became at first. It certainly wasn't easy to describe how a condom was to be used. The worst bit was to talk about that part of a man's body.

'So when a man uses it, what comes out doesn't get in,' Sofia explained.

'I just don't get this.'

'Listen to me. When a man uses one of these, nothing gets in of the stuff coming out.'

'Now you're saying something different from last time. You said "what comes out doesn't get in".'

'I know. That's what I've said all the time.'

'No you didn't. After that, you said "nothing gets in of the stuff coming out".'

'It's the same thing.'

'Either way, I still don't get it.'

'Don't you know how babies are made?'

'Of course I do. Obviously.'

'Well, the virus is in the stuff that comes out of the man. The virus can get into the woman and cause the illness. If the man you're with uses one of these, then it's less dangerous.'

'But I'm already infected.'

'Well, if whatever might come out doesn't, then it

couldn't get in either, don't you see?'

'What?'

Sofia shook her head. She didn't know how to put it any more clearly.

'The important thing is that you don't infect the men,' she said in the end. 'If you're with a man, just make him use a condom. Look, you can have my pack.'

Rosa stayed sitting on the bed, looking at Sofia.

'Have you ever done it?' she asked suddenly.

Sofia shook her head again. She could not think why Rosa had asked. Besides, if Sofia had been going out with a boy, Rosa would have known.

Rosa went out into the dark night, clutching the packet of condoms in her hand.

Sofia carried on cleaning her sewing machine. She wished the day would end soon. Rosa would still be ill tomorrow morning, but the bad day, the day they told Lydia, would at least be at an end.

Life is so strange, she thought. Why must everything be so difficult?

She decided to start again with her old habit of sitting by the fire, looking into it to find the answers to her questions. Maybe the flames would help her find explanations. It might be true that the flames are my best friends, she thought.

SIXTEEN

Exactly one month had passed since Rosa had been told about her illness. The rainy season had started. Sofia had to stay at home because she couldn't walk along the muddy road. During the last month she had been keeping her diary almost every day. By now, writing seemed as important to her as eating or sleeping.

On that day, one month after Rosa had come out from Dr Nkeka's consulting room, Sofia settled down with her diary. This is what she wrote:

I weighed myself today on Mrs Mukulela's scales, but it probably does not show the right weight. Imagine it putting up with Mrs Mukulela stepping on it every day. When Lydia is cross with her, she says that Mrs Mukulela must weigh 500 kilograms. When I have got my clothes and my legs on, I weigh 54 kilograms, but without legs it's more like 48.

Mrs Mukulela measured me with a measuring tape. Today I am 159 centimetres tall. Last time, it was 158 centimetres. I do not want to think about my height without legs, because I would be like a small child, even smaller than Alfredo.

Rosa has not got better or worse. Most days, she can work for a while, but sometimes she just wants to be left alone, sitting or lying in the shade. She has stopped going to Hassan's shop altogether. She refuses to go there, even though I am sure she longs to look at the magazines.

Lydia nags at her every day about going to visit Mr Nombora. I think she should leave Rosa alone to make up her own mind. It is she who is unwell, not Lydia. Lydia is a great mother, but I think that if I become a mother, I would try to nag as little as possible.

The boy in the road will never come back. Thinking back, I am not even sure that he is real. He might be just part of a dream, nothing more. Sometimes I can still feel him inside me. It makes me blush even when I am alone.

This has been a longer month than any other one ever. I still cannot understand how my results in the Geography test got to be so good. All the time, I keep thinking about things that have nothing to do with school. Miss Adelina is very nice to me. She started crying when I told her about the disease Rosa had caught and said that one of her brothers had it, too. She gave me a pencil when I left school that day. I would like a proper pen with ink, but it is too dear for us, even though it is not that expensive.

Lydia was very angry when she came back home yesterday, but maybe she was really more afraid than angry. Poor people are not allowed anger, only fear. A man from the capital city had come visiting. He was travelling about in a big black car with the kind of smoky windows you cannot see through. His name turned out to be Mr Bastardo, which seems just right for him. He plodded around in the field on his big feet (Lydia said that he was very fat), telling everybody there that he was planning to buy up the whole site. Lydia and the other women tried to argue with him. They said that the fields belonged to them and, besides, that working there was their only livelihood. What could they do if their land was taken away from them? This apparently made Mr Bastardo cross. He said all that was no concern of his. Lydia is still frightened that her plot of land will be taken from her. Sometimes I feel that little field is like a fine piece of jewellery to Lydia, and she fears all the time that somebody will want to steal it. As if bits of ground could be carried away by thieves, instead of always being where they are.

I have not written these last sentences as clearly as I would have liked. Maybe it is because I don't understand the ins and outs of land and ownership. Still, I cannot be bothered going back and messing about trying to get it right.

Yesterday, when I looked at my face in our mirror, I liked what I saw for the first time since Rosa fell ill. So far, all my thoughts and feelings have somehow meant that I don't care for myself, not even my own face. It was different yesterday, though. I don't know why that should be. Quite often I have been sitting by the fire in the evening, looking into it the way I used to when I was little. Not that I look for magic solutions to riddles any more, only for thoughts that might help me to answer questions like: Why did Rosa fall ill? I wonder if I will ever find out or be able to stop searching for answers.

The nicest and funniest thing that has happened this month is that Mr Temba has moved in with Mrs Mukulela. They row with each other daily, mostly about the rooster, but actually seem to enjoy each other's company very much.

Sofia wrote this in the evening, when the rest of the family was asleep. Rosa was sleeping on the floor and the light of Sofia's candle fell on her face, but she did not wake up.

Sofia had invented a secret code that she used when she wrote about things that nobody must know. If she died, she wanted some parts of her diary to be unreadable, in case somebody found it. Her system was simple enough. In the code, a sentence like 'Sometimes I can still feel him inside me' became 'Mossomeththeiggi ncaac ii feefll hmiim deedissinni emme'.

Sofia had told Rosa many times that she should move into the bed with her. Rosa insisted that she preferred sleeping on the floor.

Only once had she come to bed with Sofia. She had been very frightened that night. She thought she was going to die soon.

Sofia put her diary away and found a comfortable way to lie.

The cicadas were chirping in the dark night outside. Sometimes they sounded like an orchestra tuning up. One day, the leader of the orchestra would come and make them all play together properly.

The room was stuffy.

The window was open, but covered by a mosquito net. The net was torn in one corner and Sofia had covered the tear with bits of cloth. The rainy season brought malaria. Dangerous mosquitoes were breeding in the pools of rainwater.

She listened in the darkness and the thoughts danced in her head. Then she fell asleep.

The next morning Sofia woke with a start. It was already light outside. She did not usually sleep until this late in the morning.

Rosa was gone from beside her bed. She sat up and started strapping on her legs. There was no time to talk to Maria this morning. Why had she slept in like this?

It was raining outside and the drops were hammering on the roof of the hut.

Once her legs were on, Sofia went to the window and looked out. The road was muddy as far away as she could see. She sighed and carried on dressing. A lizard sat on the wall, watching her with his cold, round eyes.

When she was ready, she went to the door and stood there for a while. Rosa and Alfredo were busy in the cooking shed. Lydia and Faustino had left. So, Lydia had decided to walk to the *machamba* in spite of the weather. When it rained as heavily as today, working was impossible. Then Sofia realised that Lydia had gone to stand guard over her field. She must fear that if she were not there, Bastardo, or someone like him, would come driving along in his big car and take her land away from her.

Alfredo waved to Sofia, and she waved back with one of her crutches.

'Are you hungry?' Rosa called out to her. Soon afterwards, Alfredo came scuttling between the puddles in the yard, bringing her breakfast meal of corn porridge. It was hot and smelt nice. Rosa was a good cook.

Sofia pulled a stool into the doorway and settled down to eat. She was always hungry in the mornings. While she was eating, she began to get a funny feeling. She couldn't work out what it meant. The feeling had been creeping up on her at first, but was growing stronger. She remembered when she had felt the same way before: it was the day Rosa had dropped her hoe.

The feeling alerted her to something important that was about to happen. Sofia practically choked on her porridge.

Not again, she thought, full of dread. Not something else that's awful. I couldn't bear it.

This time, the feeling seemed different.

It was less overwhelming, but there was also a voice whispering inside her: Nothing awful, it said. *Something exciting will happen. Something unexpected.*

She called to Alfredo to come and get her empty plate. Rosa laughed at him as he skidded and almost fell into a puddle. Sofia was always listening out for Rosa's laugh these days. In fact, she divided life into days when Rosa laughed, and days when she did not. Days empty of laughter were always bad. Today she had laughed first thing in the morning.

146

Something unexpected, Sofia thought. And exciting.

That's just what I need on a day like this, when it's going to rain all the time. At least until tomorrow. Then the sun might shine for a bit.

She got up from the stool and went back inside the hut.

Sitting on the edge of her bed, she opened up her school books and tried to remember what they would be doing in class today. Mathematics, mostly. Sofia liked maths and was one of the very best in the class. Other pupils often came to ask her for help.

Once, when Miss Adelina had felt a little poorly and wanted to go home to lie down, she had given Sofia responsibility for taking the lessons. She was to set the class maths exercises. It had been one of the great days in Sofia's life.

A couple of weeks ago, Sofia had been at a loss to think up something to write about in her diary. In the end she decided to draw up a list of the ten best days in her life and put them in order.

The day Miss Adelina let her teach the whole class came third. Ahead of it was the day she felt she had learnt to walk properly on her prostheses. That had been amazing, especially after all those days of lying helplessly in a hospital bed.

Before both of these days came the day when Moonboy had turned up in the road outside her house.

This entry was written in her secret code. *The* best day in her life was nobody's business but her own.

Some other time, she would get a list together of the ten worst days in her life.

The day she stood on the landmine and Maria died would of course be at the top of this list. Next would come the day when she woke up in a hospital bed, racked with terrible pains, and realised that both her legs were gone.

Only there were too many bad days to choose from, even after these two. The list could become ever so long.

Sofia got on with her work. She read and did lots of maths.

She heard Rosa laugh several times while she was working in the kitchen shed. Sofia felt happy each time. The laugh was making warm feelings flow through her.

Suddenly, Rosa stood in the doorway with a parcel in her hands. It was wrapped in blue paper.

'It's for you,' she said.

'What is it?'

'I don't know.'

'Who gave it to you?'

'A girl came into the yard. She said it was for you. Some clothes that you're meant to mend.'

'What girl? What's she called?'

'Fransina. That's all I know.'

'And . . .?'

'She didn't say.'

'So how am I supposed to know whose mending I'm doing?'

'She said that you'd know.'

Sofia was surprised and baffled. She put her books away and opened the parcel. Then she became very still. She turned to stone.

Rosa looked curiously at her.

'What's the matter?' she asked.

'Nothing,' Sofia replied. 'Hey, Rosa, you'd better keep an eye on Alfredo. He might run off any minute.'

Rosa left her alone.

Sofia kept looking at the clothes in the parcel. She simply could not believe her eyes. She took a sweater from the top of the pile and buried her face in it.

It smelt of cinnamon.

SEVENTEEN

⊚⊚

That night, Sofia could not sleep at all. This time, it was not because she felt anxious. It was joyous expectation that kept her awake. During the long hours of sleeplessness, as she lay there thinking and daydreaming, there were moments when she felt ashamed of herself. She ought not to feel so happy now, when Rosa was seriously ill and one day might not be with them any more.

She couldn't help herself, though. The scent of cinnamon had been hanging heavily over the clothes in the parcel. Her Moonboy had come back.

Well, at least he had sent her a message. She kept coming back to the problem of who he might be. Still, the most important thing was that it had not all been a dream. Somewhere, he really did exist.

He had sent her a parcel of clothes to mend, so he must come and collect them. If not, he would have to ask Fransina again. She could tell Sofia who he was.

Sofia had of course gone through the clothes in the parcel. Sweaters, two shirts and one pair of trousers with a tear at the knee.

It would be easy to mend these things. She would have started straightaway if there had been any thread in her sewing kit, but she had none left after doing Mr Temba's shirts.

She twisted from side to side, unable to sleep a wink.

The rain had stopped. The frogs and cicadas were croaking and chirping away out there in the dark. A night-hunting bird cried sharply as it flew past. Then there was a long silence. Lying still was becoming too much for Sofia.

She sat up, strapped on her legs and pulled on a dress.

Lydia was snoring loudly and Sofia giggled to herself. No one could snore like Lydia.

Sofia gently pushed the door open and went outside. The yard was slippery and sticky. She took just a few steps away from the hut, prodding the ground carefully before putting her weight on a leg.

The cloud cover had split open. The moon was not yet full, but large enough for its blue rays to light the night landscape.

Sofia looked up and down the road.

It was empty, but then, she had not expected to see

him there. He had sent her a parcel. It was a promise that he would come and get the clothes one day. If he didn't, at least Sofia would find out who he was.

She wondered what his real name was. She had called him Sergio at first. Then Zé.

Lydia's snoring stopped. The door was pushed open.

Like a blue shadow, Lydia was standing in the doorway with a length of cloth wrapped round her body.

'What are you doing?' she asked.

'I couldn't sleep,' Sofia said.

'I've had such a strange dream,' Lydia said. 'It was so confusing. It started with me arriving at the *machamba* one morning and seeing a lot of monkeys sitting on the ground, champing away at my vegetables. When I tried to chase them away, they suddenly unfolded their wings and flew away. I wonder where all these crazy dreams come from,' Lydia yawned.

After a moment she looked at Sofia, thoughtfully at first, but then a smile started spreading over her face.

'Sofia, you look almost as if you were in love,' she said. 'What about that, now? It would explain your not being able to sleep. It happened to me, too, when I was your age.'

Sofia didn't answer and Lydia asked her again.

'Well, are you in love?'

'No, I'm not.'

'I think that's a fib, but I won't ask you again. If you don't want to say, that's your business.'

Lydia yawned once more and then she burst out laughing.

'I remember how it was, you know,' she said. 'I was your age when I met the man who was your father. I didn't sleep at nights either.'

Sofia would have preferred to be left alone with her thoughts. When Lydia first came out, Sofia had almost felt annoyed, but now the talk about her father interested her.

'What was it like?' she asked.

'Was what like?'

'When you met my dad?'

'I really was your age. He was not especially handsome and he always got a fit of hiccups when he was nervous.'

'Hiccups?'

'Like an old man who's had too much to drink. So you see, he was no dream prince exactly. But I liked him anyway, right from the start.'

'Why did you?'

'Because he was such a kind man. And because I didn't have to worry about him not liking me enough. That was the most important thing. Besides, his father had quite a few cows and oxen, so he wasn't poor.'

All Lydia told her was news to Sofia. She had not heard it before, nor had she thought of the time when Lydia was as young as Sofia herself.

'Which of us were you most like?' she asked. 'Me or Rosa or Maria? When you were our age?'

Lydia thought about her answer.

'You and Maria take after your father more than me,' she said. 'Rosa and I have the same face.'

'You must have been beautiful.'

Lydia stared hard at Sofia.

'What's that supposed to mean? That I'm not beautiful any longer?'

'I didn't mean that.'

'I know what you mean,' Lydia said, and laughed. 'Time passes so quickly, life runs away with you and suddenly, it seems I'm worn out. But I do remember the time when I met your father. The time when I, too, couldn't sleep.'

Sofia looked at Lydia. In the blue light of the moon, she saw her mother in a new way. The girl who had once been so young was still partly there, behind the wrinkles that told of much wear and tear.

'Maybe that was the best time in my entire life,' Lydia said. 'Except for the days when my children were born. But when you're young and in love, life is such a wonderful gift.'

Sofia wanted to know more about her father, but Lydia shook her head.

She had to go back to bed and sleep, or she wouldn't be strong enough to walk all the way to the *machamba* and back, and work there a whole day. Besides, she was going with Rosa to see Nombora, the *curandiero*. Sofia still could not make up her mind about this. Not that it mattered what she thought. It would happen the way Rosa and Lydia wanted anyway.

Lydia went indoors. Soon she started snoring again.

Sofia thought of how she must write in her diary about Lydia speaking of the man who became Sofia's father. Also, what she had said about being in love—*then life is such a wonderful gift.*

Next day she wrote:

I could not sleep last night and went outside. Frogs everywhere. Lydia came out, too. She spoke about Dad. Told me things I didn't know. When I see myself in the mirror, I am looking into his face. Lydia said that I take after him. Maria did, too. Then Lydia told me that when one is in love, life is such a wonderful gift. She didn't say who gives that gift. The answer to that mystery I must also look for in the flames of the fire.

That night, Sofia cautiously walked a little further away. She had to have a pee. She had learnt how to crouch down by holding on to the crutches and sticking one leg out straight. She didn't fall over that way. Afterwards she heaved herself upright. Sofia's arms had grown very strong.

She walked along the road.

Roads begin somewhere and end somewhere, too, she thought. People who build roads must be happy. They get to see what is on the other side of the mountains.

Suddenly she started. She stiffened with fear.

In front of her in the road was a snake. At first she had thought it was a branch but then she realised it was a snake. It was alive. She held her breath. She knew that snakes have bad eyesight. That's why you have to be very still near a snake.

But it is easier to know what you are supposed to be doing, than to actually do it. Sofia would have liked to leap backwards and hurry away.

The snake was black and almost two metres long. Sofia thought it must be a cobra. Its poison could easily kill a human being. Sofia was frightened, but forced herself to stay still. If she moved, it would dart like lightning and bite her.

What was she to do? There was nothing to do, except to stand there motionless and hope that the snake would wriggle away.

It moved. Sofia hoped it could not hear her pounding heartbeats. Then the snake stayed still. Sofia suddenly saw that its body formed a pattern. It was the letter 'N'.

Nombora, she thought. The snake has slid along the road to let me know that Nombora is waiting.

Of course she did not really want to believe that anyone could use snakes as their messengers, not even people who were said to be magicians. But she was not entirely sure.

The snake moved again and this time it slipped off the road and disappeared in the grass on the verge. Sofia drew a deep breath. Nombora is waiting for Rosa. That's how it must be, she thought.

The following morning, Alfredo was unwell. He had a sore stomach. Lydia stayed at home from the *machamba* to be with him.

'You will have to go with Rosa to Nombora's,' she told Sofia.

Sofia had not said anything about the snake she had seen on the road the night before. Could it be that Nombora had made Alfredo sick so that Lydia wouldn't be able to go with Rosa? Sofia felt uncertain about it.

It was just after ten o'clock when Rosa and Sofia set out. The sky was cloudless.

Sofia was worried about the encounter with Nombora.

EIGHTEEN

〇〇

Sofia wrote this passage in her diary before she knew that it was she who had to accompany Rosa to Mr Nombora.

I'm writing this in the morning. Rosa has not woken up yet. This morning, there was not a squeak from Mrs Mukulela's rooster. Or did I sleep so deeply that I didn't hear him? I'm not sure. Could it be that Mr Temba got his own way? Maybe he has killed the cock. I would miss it. Imagine, missing something so irritating! When I woke up I felt both sad and happy. I knew I had a dream during the night, but I can't remember it. The first thing I thought about was the snake. Was it in a dream? I ought to tell someone about it. Lydia should know, at least. Trouble is, she would just ask what I thought I was doing, walking along the wet road at night. I had better keep quiet. Must stop writing now. It is one of the days when I haven't got anything to tell myself.

The air was warm and humid.

Rosa and Sofia were walking towards Mr Nombora's place. They were both sweating. Sofia checked that the money she had brought for Mr Nombora was safe inside her blouse.

Walking with Rosa was difficult.

She changed her pace a lot. Sometimes she almost ran, and at other times her steps were slow and short. Still, Sofia said nothing. She understood that Rosa was worrying about the meeting with Mr Nombora.

These witchdoctors were hard to deal with. Sometimes they were kind, but at other times they might shout and scream. Sometimes they slapped ill people to make them better.

Suddenly Rosa stopped and wiped the sweat from her forehead.

'What were you and Lydia up to last night?' she asked.

'Did you hear us?'

'I woke and heard talking in the yard.'

'I had to go out for a pee. We just stood there for a couple of minutes watching the moon.'

'Did you talk about me?'

The question was like a blow. Rosa had spoken quickly and harshly.

'Why did you think we were talking about you?'

'You were whispering.'

'We didn't whisper. It just sounded like that because we were outside.'

Rosa was still on the attack.

'What did you say about me?'

Sofia told her the truth.

'We weren't talking about you.'

Rosa wasn't listening. She had made up her mind about what they had been saying.

'You were so. Saying that I'm going to die. That's where you're wrong. I won't die. I'll outlive the lot of you. Mr Nombora can make me well. It says so on his sign.'

Rosa's anger stunned Sofia.

It took quite a bit of thinking to work out that Rosa did not speak only from despair. She really believed in what she had said about Mr Nombora. She trusted that he would be able to cure her.

Then Sofia asked something she regretted at once.

'Why do you have to be so angry?'

Rosa stopped and stood close to Sofia.

'And if you had my disease? Wouldn't you be angry?'

Sofia wished she had never asked. But she had no time to say anything.

Rosa knocked her over. Then she took Sofia's crutches and threw them away as far as she could.

'I'm glad I'm not like you,' she screamed. 'You can only crawl without your crutches.'

Sofia felt paralysed.

Rosa had never struck her before, not even pushed her. This time was different. She had hit out intending to hurt. They had quarrelled before, but never like this.

Sofia understood that Rosa hated her.

At least, at the moment when she threw the crutches away, she was full of hatred. Then Sofia had a new insight. Rosa feared death so much that she had to have someone to hate—someone, who would live when she herself did not.

Rosa stood staring at Sofia, who was lying on the ground.

I'm the snake now, Sofia thought. A snake that Rosa would like to kill.

Rosa turned her back and walked away.

Sofia crawled across the road and into the grass where she had seen one of her crutches land. She got hold of it. Now she could stand and go looking for the other one.

The road was empty. Rosa had vanished down a slope.

Sofia wondered what she should do. Go back home or follow Rosa? She was still shaken by the attack. Still, it was Lydia who had asked her to go with Rosa to

Mr Nombora and besides, Sofia had the money.

She started walking towards Mr Nombora's place. When she passed the crest of the hill and could look down the slope, she spotted Rosa. She was sitting on a stone at the bottom of the slope with her head in her hands, rocking from side to side.

Sofia's eyes filled with tears. A human being as ill as Rosa is incurably alone. Lydia and I are there, and Alfredo and Faustino, too, but it doesn't help. Rosa is on her own.

This was an important insight.

You are alone when you face death. This was something to remember always. She would write it down in her diary.

She went up to Rosa.

'Don't say anything,' Sofia said. 'I don't need explanations.'

'I can't explain why I did that.'

'When I found out that I had no legs, I hit one of the nurses.'

When they had started walking together again, Sofia urged Rosa to hurry up. If they didn't get there in time, Mr Nombora might not receive them.

Mr Nombora lived in a hut surrounded by a tall, threatening-looking fence. It was made of corrugated iron and fortified by spiky climbers growing all over it. An ape's skull was mounted over the gateway.

When they stepped through the gate into the yard, Rosa grabbed Sofia's hand.

Inside, all seemed quiet and orderly, but still they sensed tension in the air. It was as if they had stepped into another world. A couple of women were grinding corn in a big wooden mortar. Children were running about, playing a game.

Mr Nombora was sitting on a low stool under a shady tree. He rose slowly when he saw them.

Suddenly, the whole scene in front of them became still. The children stopped playing and the women no longer worked the mortar and pestle.

Mr Nombora was tall and heavily built. His bloodshot eyes seemed to look through people. He pointed to a rug that was spread on the ground. The rug was fringed and the colour of blood. Rosa sat down on it. A younger man came running along with the stool. Mr Nombora let his massive body sink down on the stool. He put a couple of long birds' feathers in his hair. In his hand, he held a tall staff topped with a plume of long animal fur.

He started mumbling to himself. At the same time his body was rocking from side to side.

Suddenly he pointed to Sofia, who already had their

money ready in her hand. He put the money inside his shirt without looking to find out how much they had paid.

A drumbeat was starting up from somewhere. A woman was dancing. She wore a bright, blonde wig held on with a ribbon. Her feet were hammering against the ground.

This went on for almost half an hour.

Then Mr Nombora started crawling around the rug on all fours. He was mumbling, but the words were inaudible. Sometimes he seemed to be hissing like a snake. All the time, he was blowing puffs of air at Rosa.

Sofia knew what he was doing. Mr Nombora was trying to drag the evil spirits out of Rosa's body. They had been hiding in there, making Rosa ill. Not bacteria, not viruses.

Mr Nombora blew and spat, mumbled and struck out with his arms, because evil sprits were dancing in the air around him.

Rosa was sitting on the rug. She was very still and her eyes were closed.

Sofia could guess what Rosa was thinking: *Please let it be true that Mr Nombora can make me well.*

By now a thundering beat was rising from many drums and many women were dancing around the rug, their feet stamping and thumping.

Then it all stopped.

Mr Nombora sat down on his stool again, drank a couple of mouthfuls from a brown bottle and made a face.

'You have many evil spirits lodged inside your body,' he said. 'I've driven them out for now, or at least most of them. I may not have got at them all. If you don't get better, you'll have to come back to me.'

Everything had returned to normal by now. The women went on grinding corn. The children started their games again.

Rosa and Sofia left by the front gate.

'Do you feel anything?' Sofia asked.

'I'm not sure.'

They walked on in silence.

Sofia tried to work out what she thought about what had happened at Mr Nombora's place.

These evil spirits, did they really exist? Was illness something that other people wished on you, out of sheer malice? It was hard to believe.

All the same, she had better not say anything to Lydia or Rosa. They both believed in these things. Sofia herself was not sure, that was all. So, what if it were true? It might not be, but one could always hope. If Rosa got well, evil spirits were fine by Sofia.

It was a long walk back home.

Sofia felt her leg stumps begin to hurt under the straps for her prostheses. It was a familiar ache that always came on when she had been walking too far.

At least I don't get blisters on my feet, she thought. That's one good thing about not having any.

Sofia decided that she would go to bed early that evening. She was tired. Next day, she would go to school. But nothing happened the way she thought it would.

When they got back home, Lydia was there to meet them. She was very upset and spoke even faster than usual.

Mr Bastardo had come to the fields in his big car. He had shouted at her to get lost. He owned the whole site now, and would call the police if Lydia and the other women did not get off his land at once.

Lydia was in despair.

'He can't do this,' she wailed. 'How can we live without the land?'

Neither Rosa nor Sofia could answer her.

Sofia didn't sleep many hours that night. The difficulties in life never seemed to get any easier.

NINETEEN

❧

Sofia didn't get to school the next day, either. She was beginning to worry about what Miss Adelina would say. It was Lydia who had asked Sofia not to go to school.

'You speak really well,' Lydia said. 'I want you to come with me today. If Mr Bastardo has driven round and told all the women working on the *machamba* that he owns it now, they'll all be very upset. You must come and help us.'

I'm too young, Sofia thought. And I have no legs.

Lydia's problems are for grown-ups and too big for me. Rosa is ill. I just want to go to school. Why can't someone else go along and help Lydia?

The night before, the three of them had been sitting up talking until late.

Rosa told Lydia about what had happened at Mr Nombora's place.

'Do you feel better?' Lydia asked.

'I think so.'

Sofia wondered if it was true, but said nothing.

Then they talked about Mr Bastardo.

Lydia knew nothing about him, but rumour had it that he was a wealthy businessman from the capital city. Lydia came back to the same questions again and again.

'What does he want with our small plots of land? Why can't he leave us alone? How can we live if he takes our land away from us?'

Sofia suggested that Lydia should tell the village chief and ask him to help. Lydia thought it might be better to wait, and also to appeal as a group, rather than going alone. The other women must be asked to come along.

'Is it really true that people's land can be taken away just like that?' Sofia asked.

'Who cares what people like us say or think? We're poor people,' was Lydia's response.

Rosa went to bed.

'What do you think? Surely Mr Nombora helped her?' Lydia asked almost pleadingly, once Rosa had disappeared into the hut.

'We can only hope for the best,' Sofia replied evasively.

Rosa had gone to bed because she was tired. Far too tired, Sofia thought. The cold sensation in her stomach had come back.

The fire was dying down slowly. Lydia went inside.

Sofia stayed by the fire and blew on the embers to make them flare up again. She looked hard into the flames, hoping to find answers to the many questions chasing each other inside her head. Why had Rosa caught that disease? What caused some people to be poor and others to be well off?

The fire had no answers for her. It, too, slumbered in the end. All that was left were faintly glowing ashes.

Sofia undressed and crawled into bed.

As usual, Rosa was sleeping on the floor by her side. Sofia noticed that her breathing was disturbed. Then she lit her candle and pulled her diary and pencil out from under her pillow.

She was actually too tired to write, and instead tried her hand at drawing. The pencil moved across the paper almost by itself.

She discovered that she was trying to draw Lydia, but it wasn't a success. Lydia looked like an animal. Her eyes were narrow, like lines in her face, and her forehead was too high.

Sofia sighed, put the diary away and blew out the candle.

She could not sleep.

Thoughts kept rushing about and nothing could bring her peace. Rosa. Bastardo. Nombora. Over and over again.

Everything was crammed into her head.

She tried to think of other things, of the boy who would collect his clothes one day, of how he had sent her the clothes to mend. It was impossible to make her thoughts slow down and stay calm. Mr Bastardo was soon back. So was the moment Rosa dropped her hoe.

Rosa whined a little in her sleep. Sofia wondered what she was dreaming. Then other events of the day turned up in her mind. Rosa had knocked her over and thrown her crutches away. The memory still burnt hot inside her. It made her angry. Are there no limits to what a person can be allowed to do? Even someone who is very ill should not behave according to whatever came into her mind. Or maybe it was all right?

Sofia went on thinking, twisting and turning.

When Mrs Mukulela's rooster crowed in the darkness, it seemed that she had just fallen asleep. Her first thought was that Mr Temba hadn't killed the cock after all. She curled up in bed and tried to force herself back to sleep, but it didn't work. All her anxious thoughts came back to haunt her again.

That morning she went with Lydia to the *machamba*.

Rosa complained of a sore stomach, but she promised to look after both Alfredo and Faustino anyway. Lydia and Sofia left her at home.

The plots worked by the women were scattered in small squares all over a large expanse of grassland to the south of their village.

When Lydia and Sofia arrived, a group of women were already sitting on the ground near the well where they drew water for their plants. Some of their menfolk had come, too. Sofia knew most of the people there. Even though they were angry and worried, they talked and laughed a lot.

Sofia had not met many wealthy or important people in her life, but enough to make her wonder why poor people laughed much more often than the rich. Did having a large car, a grand house and lots of money go with being sour and dull? That was one more question to ask the flames in the fire at night.

The people who had gathered were very upset.

Mr Bastardo had been driving about in his big car, threatening everybody with the same outcome. If they did not do what he told them, he would get the police to arrest them. He claimed that he had bought the land and was going to start doing something with it straight-away. No one knew what exactly. One of the women had heard a rumour that he had also bought the land uphill from the field. The soil was poor there, and no good for cultivation.

Sofia listened to the talk. There were many ideas about what to do next.

In the end, everyone agreed to go together to the village chief, whose name was Ngonga. They would demand that Ngonga stop Mr Bastardo from stealing their land.

'Mr Ngonga eats the vegetables we grow here, he knows that well enough,' a woman said. She had a sharp, powerful voice.

They began a heated discussion. Could they trust Mr Ngonga? Mr Bastardo may have given him money in exchange for not protesting about the theft of their land.

Many of the women, including Lydia, were in favour of Mr Ngonga and said he was a decent man who would never do anything so dishonest. Anyway, how could Mr Bastardo buy the women's land? They had documents to prove ownership. Who could have sold land belonging to other people? The suggestions about who might have done it came thick and fast.

Sofia listened.

All thoughts of school had vanished. Listening to this discussion was education, too, in another kind of school. These people were poor but far from stupid. Sofia thought that she had rarely heard so many wise and interesting things said.

The women did most of the talking. The men were quiet and listened, making comments now and then.

Growing cereals and vegetables was women's work, Sofia thought. Their labour produces food for everyone, the men, too.

The talk was slowing. A small, slender woman called Ruth turned to Sofia and looked at her.

'You go to school,' she said. 'You can read and write, unlike most of us. What do you think we should do?'

Sofia shook her head to distance herself from the question.

'I have nothing to add,' she said.

Lydia wasn't pleased.

'Can't you think of anything to say? What's all this schooling for then?'

This annoyed Sofia. She didn't show it, but she thought that at times Lydia said the most stupid things, which she probably didn't mean.

'I think you've made the right decision,' she said. 'Talk to Mr Ngonga about this. If he wants his food tomorrow, he has to stop Mr Bastardo from stealing the land.'

'If it doesn't work, there is nothing left for us except to defend our land,' one of the women said. She had been silent until then. 'We must be prepared to stand guard at night, too. Otherwise he might come along with big machines and rip out all our plants.'

Sofia accompanied the procession of women and men to Mr Ngonga's place.

Her legs were badly chafed now and her stumps ached. It was such an effort to walk all the way that she got a nose-bleed. She tore pieces off her *capulana* and stuffed them into her nostrils.

They stopped outside Mr Ngonga's hut.

Mr Ngonga knew they were coming, because they had been singing.

> *We want to keep our land,*
> *That's all we have got.*
> *It's not for Mr Big-Car Bastardo,*
> *We want to keep our land . . .*

They sang these words over and over again.

Lydia and some of the other women pushed Sofia to the front.

Was she meant to speak for them? She had not expected this. Besides, she looked silly. Why should Mr Ngonga listen to a girl with two bits of cloth stuck up her nostrils?

'Please, let somebody else speak,' Sofia pleaded.

'You're the best at it,' a woman called Joanna said.

Sofia leaned on her crutches. Mr Ngonga looked at her kindly.

'Well now, Sofia. Sofia Alface Fumo,' he said. 'You've

grown since last time I saw you. What do you want? I heard the song about your land. And about someone called Mr Bastardo.'

Sofia explained and Mr Ngonga listened without interrupting her. She could hear encouraging remarks muttered and whispered by the women behind her.

Sofia fell silent. Mr Ngonga scratched his bald head.

'No one can take your land away from you,' he said. 'I'll investigate this Mr Bastardo to find out who he is and what kind of claim he could possibly have to the fields. I promise you that nobody will steal your land.'

When they heard this, the women cheered Mr Ngonga. Some of them started dancing in front of him.

'I told you that you're a good talker,' Lydia said proudly.

'You could have said what I did just as well,' Sofia replied. 'You would probably have said it better.'

The women returned to their *machambas*.

Sofia went home. It was afternoon already. She was tired but her nose-bleed had stopped.

When Sofia turned into their yard, Alfredo was sitting on the ground, drawing in the sand. Faustino was sleeping on a length of cloth spread out next to Alfredo.

'Where's Rosa?' Sofia asked in surprise.

Alfredo pointed towards the hut.

175

Sofia went inside.

Rosa was lying on the mat on the floor next to the bed. She was awake and looked at Sofia with frightened eyes.

Sofia felt Rosa's forehead. It was hot. She also noticed that there was a small sore near one of Rosa's ears.

The cold lump in Sofia's stomach was back at once. Mr Nombora's ministrations had not helped Rosa. She was worse and more ill now than ever before.

TWENTY

๏

Two evenings later, Sofia wrote in her diary:

Rosa is ill now. Very ill. She no longer has the strength to do anything, even get up from the floor. I have tried to make her lie in the bed. She doesn't want to. It's as if she feels more at home on the floor. Lydia and I have to take turns to help her when she needs to have a pee or the other thing (that is often, because her stomach is upset all the time). She has no appetite. When I washed her because she was sweating so much, I discovered sores all over her body. I asked why she hadn't told us about them. She said that she had not wanted to. Maybe she felt ashamed. Anyway, what could I have done? I cannot think what. Rosa is beginning to take in that she will die. She says nothing. I can see it though. It's inside her. Death is in her eyes, like a shadow. Lydia is in despair and so am I. Lydia has so many other things on her mind that I have to care for Rosa.

I walked to school today and had a talk with Miss Adelina. I told her everything, just the way it is. She was very sorry. Then she said I must come back, but only when I felt it was right. When will that be? I dare not think about the answer. It could be that I can't go back to school until Rosa has died. I have never felt as lonely as I do now. Not even when I was in hospital and thought about how both my legs were gone and Maria was dead. Rosa simply must not die. I can't bear this. Lydia has no strength left. Why is there no one to help her?

When Sofia had finished talking with Miss Adelina, she went to the health centre. The nurse was sitting there as she always seemed to be, swatting flies and filling in papers. She was just about to close the centre. All the patients who had come that morning had been seen and gone home.

'Has Dr Nkeka left?' Sofia asked.

'He's not seeing any more patients today.'

'I'm not ill. I just wanted to ask him something.'

The nurse looked her up and down.

'I recognise you,' she said. 'You've got a sister who's ill. Isn't that right?'

'Yes it is.'

The nurse rose and knocked on the door to the doctor's room. Dr Nkeka came out. He was no longer wearing his white doctor's coat. When he saw Sofia, he nodded at her to come in. Sofia sat down on a chair in front of his desk.

Sofia thought that Rosa must have been sitting on this chair when she learnt that she had caught that serious illness.

'How's your sister?' Dr Nkeka asked.

Sofia didn't want to cry, but she just couldn't stop herself. She burst into tears. Dr Nkeka sat silently looking at her. Then he gave her a handkerchief and she dried her eyes.

'I understand that she's already very ill,' Dr Nkeka said.

'She can't get up any more,' Sofia said. 'There are sores all over her body. Her stomach is always upset.'

Dr Nkeka nodded. He did not seem at all surprised.

'Is there nothing we can do for her?'

There was no question more important than this simple one. Sofia had come to the health centre to hear the answer.

'No,' Dr Nkeka said. 'I speak to you as I would to an adult. Well, you are an adult. Going through something like losing one's legs, like you did, makes one grow up very quickly. So I'll tell you the truth as precisely as I can and not try to sound hopeful to make things easier for you. There is nothing anyone can do for your sister. She's beyond the infected stage and has already developed the full-blown disease. That's why her stomach causes her so much trouble. It's also the cause of all those sores. I can prescribe medication to help her cope with the symptoms, but there's no cure for the disease itself. It makes this condition so particularly dreadful. There's no cure. All anyone can do is take care not to get infected. I assume you know about the most common way to catch the infection?'

Sofia knew.

'Just now, during the few minutes we're sitting here talking together, other young people are catching the infection,' Dr Nkeka said. 'In this country, three hundred young people, under the age of twenty, catch the infection every day. I can't stop thinking about it all the time. What to do? Most of them are poor. They can't read or write. How to reach them and explain to them about the disease and the importance of protecting themselves against it? At times I despair, terribly.'

Dr Nkeka fell silent. Then he sighed and got up from his chair.

'I must go now,' he said. 'There's one more health centre to attend before the evening.'

He went over to a cupboard, took out two jars and showed them to Sofia. One of them contained an ointment for Rosa's sores and the other was full of tablets, which would soothe her upset stomach.

Then Dr Nkeka picked up his doctor's bag from the floor.

'Where do you live?' he asked.

Sofia explained.

'Really? And you walk that distance and back every day?' Dr Nkeka looked at her in amazement.

'I can't get to school any other way,' Sofia said.

They left the health centre together. The nurse had gone already. Dr Nkeka nodded goodbye to the old man who kept watch over the empty building.

'I'll drive you home,' Dr Nkeka said. He walked along to an ancient-looking car parked in the yard. One of the headlamps was gone. The rear window was covered in cardboard instead of glass.

'People imagine that doctors are well off,' Dr Nkeka said. 'True, some are. That's if you're looking after people with lots of money. But doctors like me, who spend their time travelling between rural health centres, we have to be content with cars like this. We can't afford anything better. Come on, let's see if it will start.'

Dr Nkeka laughed when he said that.

Sofia climbed into the front passenger seat. The springs were so weak that she almost sank to the floor. Dr Nkeka turned the ignition key. The engine coughed, but turned over and started. Sofia gave directions, and off they went.

'I was born round here,' Dr Nkeka told her. 'I was determined to become a doctor. Nobody believed I would succeed.'

Sofia listened with great interest. She had the same dream as Dr Nkeka had once had, and he had made it come true.

'Is it possible to become a doctor if you don't have any legs?' she asked.

Dr Nkeka looked at her, surprised at her question. 'Of course you can. Do you want to train in medicine?'

Sofia did not say anything more and Dr Nkeka did not ask any more questions.

He drove her all the way home. He also took the time to go into the hut and visit Rosa. He mustn't tell her that she will die, Sofia thought anxiously.

But Dr Nkeka said nothing like that. He looked at Rosa's sores, felt her forehead and asked her how she was.

Afterwards, when he had driven away, Sofia thought that he might have tried to encourage Rosa. Still, he had not said anything that wasn't true and had not given her any false expectations.

Sofia dragged her sewing machine out into the yard. She started to mend the clothes in the parcel. Faustino was awake and Sofia tied him on to her back. She wondered if one day she would carry her own child on her back and not just a little brother.

Alfredo liked watching Sofia working the sewing machine. His eyes kept following the needle as it moved quickly up and down. She had started with the tear in the knee of the trousers, but first she let Alfredo sniff the trousers. She smiled.

'What's that smell, do you know?' she asked.

'Cinnamon,' Alfredo said, and smiled back at her.

So it's not my imagination, Sofia thought quietly to herself. This pair of trousers really does belong to the boy I met in the road in the moonlight.

Then she remembered how he had taken his trousers off. This made her feel both embarrassed and excited.

Mr Temba came walking across the yard. He bowed to her.

'I believe that Rosa is ill,' he said. 'I do hope it's nothing serious?'

'She's very ill,' Sofia said. 'I don't know how serious it is.'

The last bit was untrue.

Sofia felt that she could not tell Mr Temba the truth. He loved gossip. Mrs Mukulela was just like him. If it was a fact that the two of them had got together, the entire village would know everything Sofia said about Rosa before the day was over.

'Mrs Mukulela has been most pleasant to me recently,' Mr Temba said.

'I know,' Sofia replied.

Mr Temba seemed astonished.

'Has Mrs Mukulela spoken about this?'

'About what?'

'About us two?'

'Please, Mr Temba,' Sofia said. 'I haven't got any legs, but I have eyes.'

She really shouldn't speak to Mr Temba like that. Maybe he'd take offence. But she knew that Mr Temba liked her and they often shared a joke together.

'It's bad for a man to be alone,' Mr Temba said thoughtfully. 'But then, it's no good for a woman, either.'

Then he doffed his hat to her and left.

Sofia got on with her sewing.

When she had finished mending the trousers, she started on the most badly frayed of the shirts. All the time she was working, she kept thinking about what Dr Nkeka had said.

There was no cure for Rosa. She really would die. It was still very hard for Sofia to believe that this was true. The icy feeling in her stomach came and went. Sometimes tears dripped from her eyes. Still, she gritted her teeth and carried on sewing.

Nothing would improve if she lay down on the ground and did what she wanted to do—scream wildly, over and over again. The fire must help me, she thought. What is the point of Rosa dying? Why are the rest of us alive?

There must be answers. Riddles may be hard to crack, but still it can be done.

Sofia sewed.

Now she was worrying about what it would be like when Lydia came home. She must be told what Dr Nkeka had said.

Sofia knew perfectly well that Lydia would refuse to believe there was no cure. Mr Nombora was not the only *curandiero* around. There were others, and Lydia would turn to them. She would do everything in her power to prevent Rosa's death. Anything.

Lydia was coming along the road.

She carried a huge bundle of branches on her head— firewood for their cooking. Sofia ached inside. She had to tell Lydia, now.

How to say something she couldn't say? Something she did not dare to say.

Lydia put down the bundle and stretched her back.

'We've agreed to stand guard,' she said.

'Every night. Mr Bastardo won't be able to take us by surprise.'

'But Mr Ngonga told you there was no need to worry.'

'Poor people always need to worry,' Lydia replied. 'Don't forget that. Ever.'

Sofia promised her not to forget.

Lydia lifted Faustino from Sofia's back. Then she started to kindle the fire. Sofia folded up the clothes she had been working on and dragged the sewing machine back inside.

Rosa was asleep. Sweat glistened on her forehead and she had thrown off her blanket. Her body was almost covered with sores now. Sofia went outside.

Lydia was grinding corn.

'How's Rosa?' she asked.

Sofia took a deep breath. Then she told her mother the truth.

Rosa would die soon.

TWENTY-ONE

The sound was of an animal in dreadful pain.

Sofia had never experienced anything like this. Nothing so frightening.

Lydia howled. The howl came from deep inside her body and rose to emerge from her mouth in a long ululation.

Mrs Mukulela came hurrying to find out what had happened. In her anxiety to get there she moved as fast as her heavy body would let her. Mr Temba, who had been sitting outside his hut with his baskets, got up and disappeared through his doorway.

Sofia's eyes were registering everything that happened.

Soon Mr Temba would come outside wearing his hat. He went nowhere without a hat on his head. Even when Death came to take him away, Mr Temba would apologise for the delay and go to get his hat.

Sofia was taking it all in, and in front of her was Lydia, howling.

Sofia had told her precisely what the situation was. Rosa would die from the disease. Because she was getting worse so quickly, it would soon be all over. Dr Nkeka had no doubts about Rosa's condition. He had also taken the trouble to visit Rosa, see her inside the hut and examine her sores.

Lydia, who had been so steadfast all the time and so determined to find a cure, suddenly gave up. Sofia had not thought of the possibility that Lydia would react like this. Of course she realised that Lydia would take it badly. She would be very sad and very frightened, but continue to look for solutions the way she always did.

Instead Lydia collapsed.

Sofia felt that she would never forget the way Lydia sank to the ground, as if she wanted to sink into the earth and disappear. It was as if a sudden dreadful blow had cut open her body and caused all her strength to drain away.

A woman who has just learnt that her child will die looks like this, Sofia told herself. It doesn't matter that Lydia has experienced this before. Every time is the first time.

'What's going on?' Mrs Mukulela asked, sounding alarmed. Almost at the same time, she spotted some curious boys, who had stopped in the road to look, and shouted to them to get lost, at once.

188

Lydia shook her head. She could not speak.

Sofia explained.

Now Mr Temba had arrived. When he heard that Rosa was very ill and would die soon, he took his hat off.

'It's so wicked to make evil spirits enter someone like Rosa, it's hard to believe,' Mrs Mukulela said, and suddenly seemed very scared. 'A young girl who's done no harm.'

'It's not evil spirits,' Sofia said. 'It's an illness.'

'All illnesses are caused by evil spirits,' Mrs Mukulela said sharply, as if Sofia needed a telling off.

Sofia didn't reply. She knew that Mrs Mukulela was convinced, like most of the other village people, that there was no explanation for illness except that evil spirits had taken possession of the body.

'This is terrible to hear,' Mr Temba said. 'I have heard of this disease. It creeps into people but it doesn't show, and can't be detected until it suddenly saps all their strength.'

Lydia was sitting on the ground, bowed and silent.

She is like a lost child, Sofia thought. And I can't help her.

Mrs Mukulela cooked supper because Lydia was too weak.

Mr Temba sat down by the fire and shared their meal. Sofia kept looking into the flames. She needed more and more answers, because the questions kept crowding into her mind. She could not concentrate properly, though. She needed to be alone with the fire.

All the time, Rosa slept.

Later, Lydia sat by her side and spread Dr Nkeka's ointment all over her daughter's body. The candle was lit. Sofia stood in the doorway and watched Lydia moving in the dark shadows of the room. The evening wind caused a draught through the broken window and made the shadows flicker and shift.

Lydia was whispering and mumbling as she gently covered the many dark red wounds with the ointment. Sofia could not make out the words and thought that Lydia might be saying prayers. Prayers to whatever gods there might be. None of them ever came to the rescue when you really needed them.

That was another huge riddle. The riddle of the gods.

Afterwards Lydia was utterly exhausted.

'I should have been on guard at the fields tonight, but I haven't got the strength to go.'

Did she mean that Sofia should take Lydia's place? Sofia was not sure, and Lydia said nothing more. She put the ointment away and then went to lie down on the floor in the other room, where Alfredo and Faustino were already asleep.

Sofia went to bed. She was so weary and bone-tired that she fell asleep at once. Then the dreams came sneaking out from the dark corners in her mind.

Over the last year or so, Sofia had started to imagine the inside of her head as a kind of landscape. The dreams themselves had different settings and might take place at night or during the day. Sometimes the moon and the stars shone, but the dream-sky could also be covered with heavy, grey clouds. It might rain in her dreams. Anything might happen.

Her memories were hiding behind trees and shrubs. She never knew which ones would suddenly leap out. Anything might happen in the landscapes of her dreams.

It was still dark when Sofia woke. Mrs Mukulela's rooster had not started crowing yet.

Sofia wrote down her dream:

I am standing in a road. It is evening. I am on my way to some place, but I don't know where. Suddenly a man turns up in front of me. He has a mask over his face but in spite of that I don't feel afraid of him. His mask is made of leather. It's dark but I can still see that the mask is red and yellow and black. There are greyish-white hairs sticking out from its sides and teeth in the opening for the mouth. The teeth might belong to the mask or to the face behind it. I can't tell. I'm not even sure if the mask looks threatening or kind.

Then I understand that it is Death who stands there.
Still I am not afraid.

Then I woke up. The man with the mask had come
to get Rosa, but he was too early. She is breathing,
asleep down there on the floor.

Sofia reached out her hand and felt Rosa's forehead. It
was still hot.

Rosa was alive. Feeling Sofia's hand searching her face
made her restless. She started mumbling in her sleep.
Sofia tried to catch what she was saying. It was as if Rosa
was trying to free herself from something.

Sofia felt an icy hand grip her heart. Rosa isn't fighting to
escape dying, she thought. She is fighting to get away
from her terror. Her fear of dying, of not living. Of being
denied a whole, long life.

Sofia had to press both her hands against her mouth
to stop herself from screaming. Dark riddles everywhere.
No answers. Why? Why the silence, even in the fire? If
not even the flames could tell her the truth, who could?

Rosa calmed down again. Then Sofia heard Mrs
Mukulela's rooster, sounding almost sad in the dark.

Maybe it knows that it's taking a dangerous risk, Sofia
thought. It might understand that the people who've
woken up feel ready to kill it there and then.

She strapped on her legs, got up, dressed and went out-side. The darkness was warm and humid. She looked towards the road. No boy. Nothing.

There was nothing she wanted to do except scream. Shatter the dark with her voice.

But she was silent, just stood there, very still, thinking that a miracle might happen. That Rosa might get up again and be well. That it might all be just a terrible nightmare.

Slowly it became light.

First, an almost invisible line of faint, grey light. Next, the sun came rolling up over the horizon. The birds woke, then the human beings.

Lydia came out into the yard.

Sofia noted how worn her clothes looked. This shamed her. She should have mended Lydia's clothes.

'We've got to take Rosa to another doctor,' Lydia said. 'Of course there must be a cure for her illness.'

Sofia could hear that Lydia was determined. She never gave in, for as long as there was any hope left for a child of hers. It was never too late.

Although Lydia was tired, she tied Faustino to her back and walked away along the road. As usual, she walked quickly. She was in a hurry.

Alfredo asked if he could go and play with some

friends. Sofia nodded and told him not to be away for long.

Sofia went inside the hut. Rosa was awake.

'Do you want something to eat?' Sofia asked.

'I'm not hungry.'

'Come on, you must eat.'

'I'm not hungry.'

Sofia gave her a mug of tea and left her. That was the last of the tea leaves. The jar was empty and they had no money to buy more. All the money Sofia had got from Mr Temba had been spent on paying Mr Nombora. Not that it had made any difference.

Sofia lifted down the piece of mirror and examined her face. She could see how tired she looked. She put the mirror back again.

At that moment, Mr Temba came walking along, greeted her and bowed.

'I couldn't sleep last night,' he said. 'I couldn't stop thinking of Rosa, all night long. Mrs Mukulela has also been thinking about your sister. We decided not to sleep in the same house last night because of this. We both wanted to be alone while we were thinking about Rosa.'

Mr Temba sat down on the stool next to the kitchen shed.

'I have understood this much: the infection might

come if you care very much for someone,' he said. 'When you sleep together and your love for each other is strong. Young people need love. So do those of us who've grown older. Isn't it true that once Rosa had a boyfriend called Steven? I've forgotten his surname.'

'Gomane,' Sofia said.

Mr Temba nodded thoughtfully. 'And, am I misinformed or did Steven Gomane work in the South African mines for some time?'

'He worked there for two years.'

Mr Temba nodded again. Sofia knew that he wanted to tell her something. She waited.

'I recalled that I had some news of Steven Gomane recently,' he finally said.

'What was the news, Mr Temba?'

He was looking at her as he replied. 'The news was that Steven Gomane died fairly recently. And that the cause of death was this dreadful disease that cannot be cured.'

Mr Temba rose, bowed and went back to the waiting baskets outside his hut.

Sofia thought about what he had said, and about Rosa, alone on the floor in there.

TWENTY-TWO

That day, Sofia spent a lot of time looking for a laugh.

When Mr Temba had left, she felt completely woebe-gone. She thought that she had to experience something that would give her pleasure. She couldn't go without any more.

She had to laugh, at least once in the morning and once at night. If not, her whole life would come apart.

But where would you go looking for a laugh? Where was the run-away laugh hiding? She thought that this was a childish notion—a run-away laugh. Still, she wanted to be childish and no one was to stop her.

She walked along the road and turned on to a path leading to a hut with a broken roof.

In the hut lived one of Lydia's cousins, or maybe a cousin-twice-removed. Her name was Graçieta.

Sofia was not sure what kind of relation Graçieta was

but they were related, that much was certain. She had a lot of children and a man who came to see her once a year. Sofia had met him. Every time he came to stay with Graçieta, he went the rounds of all the relatives. His name was Ricardo. He was very short. Unlike Ricardo, Graçieta was tall. She had a prominent, plump bottom and liked wriggling it.

Ricardo's reason for being away so much was that he earned his money working as a street shoemaker in a distant city, all the way down by the South African border. He saved as much of his earnings as he could. Then he went home to Graçieta, gave her the saved-up money and stayed with her for a few days before going away again. Nine months later Graçieta would give birth to another baby. This happened the same way, year after year.

Just thinking of Graçieta and her bouncy bum made Sofia laugh. Most people, like Sofia, laughed with their mouths, but Graçieta laughed with her big bottom.

Sofia stopped. It had been easier than she had thought to find a laugh. She decided to walk on, having got this far. She would visit Graçieta, and tell her that Rosa was ill.

Graçieta was cutting her toenails when Sofia turned up. Because she was so tall, it was quite complicated for her to get at her toes with her rusty pair of scissors. She had propped herself up against the wall of the hut and pushed against it while she had one leg up on a stool. Then she tried to reach down with the scissors.

She beamed at Sofia.

'Here's the girl who's come to save me!' she shouted.

Sofia couldn't recall ever having met anyone who spoke as loudly as Graçieta. Sometimes people would tell her to be a bit quieter.

'I *am* quiet,' she would roar. Nobody would bother to protest. Obviously, it was pointless. She simply couldn't lower her voice.

'Can't get at my nails,' she shouted. 'You must help me.'

Sofia grabbed the blunt scissors and started to trim Graçieta's toenails. They were as hard as stone, but Sofia had strong hands and arms. Soon she had finished the job. Graçieta scrutinised her large feet. She was very pleased.

'You see, Ricardo's on his way,' she told Sofia. 'He's got the right to find his wife with trimmed nails. Besides he hates it if my nails scratch him when he and I make another baby.'

Sofia should have been used to Graçieta's frank way of talking about these things, but it was still embarrassing.

There was no part of what might take place between a man and a woman that Graçieta wouldn't speak about,

198

she thought. Shout about. Everybody within earshot knew by now that Ricardo was on his way, and why it was important that Graçieta's nails were properly cut.

Graçieta asked how the family was.

'Rosa is ill,' Sofia said. 'Very seriously ill.'

'Ill?' Graçieta cried. 'Really? Ill with what?'

Sofia wondered how she could avoid letting the whole neighbourhood know that Rosa was so ill that she was going to die soon. Even if she suggested that they should talk more inside the hut, Graçieta's mighty voice would be heard right through the mud walls.

'Her stomach is upset all the time,' Sofia said. 'She's got fever. Dr Nkeka says there is no cure for her disease.'

'Oh my God, she's got AIDS,' Graçieta screamed, and began to sigh and rock her big body from side to side.

Sofia saw that she was truly saddened.

Rosa had told her that when Maria had died and Sofia was in hospital after the accident, Graçieta had been a real support for Lydia.

'So many are dying,' Graçieta cried. 'This disease will empty our villages. Soon there'll only be children and old folk left. What will happen then?'

Sofia had no answers. She was just glad that Graçieta existed. She was good to be with, no matter if one was happy or sad. She would surely help Lydia again when it became necessary.

Sofia walked home afterwards. Rosa was awake, but still refused food.

'Do you want me to stay here with you?' Sofia asked.

'No. Where's Lydia?'

Sofia looked wonderingly at Rosa. She should know that Lydia was working on the *machamba* as usual. Rosa's eyes looked shiny and blank. Sofia thought that she might not be aware what time of day it was.

'She'll be back soon,' Sofia said.

'I want my mummy to be here,' Rosa mumbled. 'I want my mummy to be here.'

Sofia dragged the sewing machine into the yard and went on mending the Moonboy's clothes.

Thinking about him, she gave him a new name. Moonboy didn't seem satisfying any more. What about Cinnamonboy? That's his name now. The idea made her giggle.

She couldn't help wondering why she was sent his worn clothes. Did he know that she had a sewing machine? Someone must have told him. Who could it have been?

Sofia kept sewing. She was dreaming at the same time. Daydreaming:

Rosa's illness had gone. So had Lydia's fear of Mr Bastardo. Sofia herself had grown up. She was married, owned her house and had many children. Rosa and

Lydia would visit her. Alfredo and Faustino would have grown up, too. There was a wide veranda along the front of Sofia's house. Inside there might even be electric light. Cinnamonboy was a schoolteacher or maybe an important politician, who travelled everywhere in a car bigger than Mr Bastardo's. Sofia was a doctor. Everybody knew who she was, because she had discovered the cure for the serious illness.

That was where the dream came apart.

She could not make it last any longer. It was impossible to think the real Rosa away for any length of time.

She carried on sewing.

Alfredo came home. He had fallen and cut his knee. Sofia cleaned it with some water. He didn't complain, even though it hurt.

'What's wrong with Rosa?' he asked suddenly.

Sofia saw that he was serious, and fearful of the answer. She and Lydia had both forgotten about Alfredo. He was there, watching and listening, taking note of everything. It was just that he didn't say much. They shouldn't have forgotten to explain to him why Rosa never ate anything and just lay on the floor inside the hut all the time.

'Rosa is ill,' she said. 'Very seriously ill.'

'Will she die?' The question was produced without any hesitation. Alfredo had prepared it carefully and waited

201

for the right moment to ask.

'Rosa will get better,' Sofia said.

Alfredo didn't say anything more. He settled down near the kitchen shed and started drawing with a stick in the sand. Alfredo was just a small boy, but nobody knew better how to shelter himself inside silence.

Why did I lie? Sofia asked herself. Why not tell him the truth?

She started working at the sewing machine again. There were two more shirts left to mend. The needle snagged. She hit the sewing machine irritably. The needle was causing her trouble to let her know she had been wrong not to tell Alfredo the truth. It was punishing her.

'I shall tell him what it's really like,' she whispered to the sewing machine. 'I was wrong, but I'll make it right now.'

She discovered that a few grains of sand had jammed the aperture through which the needle moved up and down. She turned the wheel gently and the needle worked free.

She rose and went across to Alfredo.

He had drawn a face in the sand. It was Rosa's face.

'Rosa is very ill,' Sofia said. 'She might die.'

Alfredo went on drawing. He said nothing.

The afternoon came, bringing the short hours of twilight.

Sofia finished mending the last of the shirts and dragged the sewing machine back inside the hut. Rosa was asleep, or maybe she was just pretending, so that she would be left in peace. Sofia was not sure.

When she went out into the yard, Lydia had just arrived. She was angry and fearful.

'That Mr Bastardo is driving about in his car,' she said, and her voice was shaking. 'People are saying there's a large digger on its way. We'll have to be on guard again tonight.'

'Rosa is asking for you,' Sofia said. By now she couldn't care less about Mr Bastardo.

Lydia went into the hut. Sofia got the fire going and started making supper. Their stores were almost empty. Just a little corn left. Hardly any vegetables.

Lydia came outside and sat down. Her appetite seemed to have gone.

'We've got to get her to another doctor,' Lydia said. 'I've heard of a very skilful *curandiero* in Xai-Xai. But how on earth am I going to find the money for the bus tickets?'

Evening came and darkness fell.

Lydia got up.

'I've got to go to the *machamba*,' she said. 'I won't be back until tomorrow evening.'

She went into the hut to say goodbye to Rosa. Sofia

203

heard a sudden scream. It was Rosa. She went to the door to listen. Alfredo was scared. He stood next to Sofia and held her hand hard.

Rosa didn't want Lydia to leave her.

Sofia went inside. Rosa was holding on to Lydia's arms and did not want to let go.

She was screaming that she didn't want to die. Above all, though, she didn't want Lydia to leave her alone. Sofia went up to the curtain.

'I'll go to the *machamba*,' she said. 'It's much better that you're at home.'

It was dark when Sofia arrived and a thunderstorm was rumbling in the distance.

Just where the road entered the fields, a large fire had been lit. The women sitting around the fire were talking and laughing together. Sofia stood in the dark without letting them know that she was there. She thought of how, some time in the future, she would be one of them. Guarding fields by the fire, talking and laughing. Rocking children to sleep.

That is, unless she succeeded in becoming a doctor. She saw one possibility for her life in front of her. It was a life that could have been Rosa's.

She cracked down on that thought, broke it like a dry branch. She no longer had the strength to think about Rosa, not now.

She went over to the fire and felt part of the community. It was a good, secure feeling.

The talk was lively. Angry words about Mr Bastardo. Or maybe they were all frightened? Then rude jokes about what all these crazy men were up to. Sofia had heard it all before, but it made her happy to hear it again.

One by one, the women curled up and fell asleep.

They had agreed on a guard roster. Sofia was lying on her back with her crutches under her head, staring up at the night sky. The stars looked back down at her.

When she woke up she remembered dreaming about Mr Temba. He had made a special basket that had grown wings and flown away, to the amazement of all.

I'm dreaming about wings, Sofia said to herself. About wings and flying away. Maybe it's my legs I'm really dreaming about. Not to fly, but to walk and feel the blood flowing strongly, all the way down into my feet.

Now it was her turn to keep watch. Sofia threw some branches on the fire and her eyes were drawn to the flames. They still held no answers to her questions.

She got up, yawned and walked over to the roadside. It was a still night. A dog was barking somewhere in the distance. Then silence closed in again.

At first, it was like a distant rumble. Faint but growing stronger. The headlamps were visible far away, down at the bottom of the slope by the river.

Now she could see what it was. Like a giant insect, a large digger was crawling up towards her.

TWENTY-THREE

⊚⊚

Sofia shouted to the women to wake up.

Still drowsy, they hurried to get ready, pulled their wraps tight around their bodies and gathered by the road.

The sky was growing light. It was morning already. The giant insect was spewing out black exhaust and crawling slowly closer.

The women were anxiously discussing what to do next. Someone suggested they should take all their clothes off and lie down naked in the road. Someone else said that they should throw stones at the digger. Feverishly, Sofia tried to think what was the best course. What would Lydia have done? Sofia was there in her place. It followed that she should do what Lydia would have done.

The great insect stopped crawling, and stayed still, watching them with its cold shining headlamp-eyes. A black car drove up and parked next to the insect. Mr Bastardo stepped out and walked towards the women.

'So you're still here!' he shouted. 'I've bought this site. It's mine. Get the hell out!'

The women responded with furious questions and assertions.

'So what are we to do? How do we live? It's our land. We've got the documents.'

'I'm a very important, powerful man,' Mr Bastardo shouted back at them. 'Your papers are worthless. This land is mine. If you don't get the hell out now I'll call the police. You'll be in prison tonight, every one of you!'

At this point, he waved a small telephone in the air. Sofia had heard somewhere that nowadays there were telephones without wires. So was it true? Was Mr Bastardo about to call the police?

The women carried on pouring out their protests. What would they live on?

The man in the road didn't listen.

'Get lost! Go!' he shouted. 'I won't have my plans messed up by a bunch of screaming bitches. You've got three minutes to get away from here.'

Mr Bastardo waved at the man driving the digger. It started crawling again.

What would Lydia have done? Sofia asked herself. Just now, at this moment?

Images were rushing through her head:

Lydia carrying her hoe. Faustino tied to her back.

Every day. Year after year. Off to the *machamba*, to sow and to harvest, to watch over the corn and the vegetables. *Their lifeline.*

The insect was coming closer. Mr Bastardo was standing at the side of the road. He was laughing.

Sofia grabbed a firm hold of her crutches and walked out to the road. Right out into the middle, into the path of the crawling insect.

Mr Bastardo was still laughing. The women were shouting.

The insect was getting closer and closer. The dawn had broken but the headlamp-eyes were still glaring at her.

Her heart was thumping in her chest. She was scared. Still, she had no intention of moving. She would stand there until that thing ran over her.

The insect screeched. The man had blown the horn. By now Mr Bastardo had stopped laughing. He was shouting at her to get out of the way.

Sofia stood still where she was. She did not move at all. The insect slowed its crawling. It screeched again.

The women were screaming. Mr Bastardo ran to Sofia and tried to push her down. She struck him then, with one of her crutches. He lifted his hand to hit her.

Now all the women screamed in unison and rushed out into the road.

The insect had stopped, just a metre or two away from Sofia. People were running in all directions.

Mr Bastardo was wiping the sweat off his face. He had become hoarse from all the shouting. The man in the digger looked scared. The road was full of people. Mr Bastardo realised that the air was full of menace. Someone threw a stone at his car.

'I'll be back,' he shouted. 'With the police.'

Another stone hit his car.

Mr Bastardo called out to the man driving the digger, leapt into his car and drove off. The insect started crawling backwards, very slowly at first. The women were cheering.

Sofia was shaking now. She had to sit down on a stone by the roadside. She had done something she didn't actually dare to do.

I must write this in my diary, she thought. It's possible to do things that you don't dare to do.

One of the women came and gave her a mug of water.

'That was very brave of you,' she said.

'I wasn't brave,' Sofia replied. 'I only did what Lydia would have done.'

The feelings among the people in the road were still running high. Mr Bastardo had threatened them. He would be back and bring police officers with him. Still, all those who had gathered there were totally united.

Mr Bastardo would not get their land. He could bring as many policemen as he liked.

Sofia walked back home. The day was growing hotter already. She walked slowly. What had happened seemed to be changing into a memory of a strange dream.

Sofia was convinced that Mr Bastardo would be back. Maybe he would come accompanied by policemen. She was also certain that the women would put up a fight. They would not let anyone take their land away. It was no different from taking their lives. During the day, everyone in villages around here would learn what had happened. Now nobody would hesitate about standing in the way of Mr Bastardo and his digger, should he try to come back.

Sofia stopped. One of the straps holding her legs in place had worked loose.

A terrible thought struck her. What if Rosa had died? Maybe she had known that her end was near and that was why she wanted Lydia to stay close to her.

Sofia hurried now. After a while, the strap of her leg worked loose again. She swore, tightened it and walked on. The thought that Rosa might have died made her feel panicky.

When she got back home, she saw to her relief that Rosa was still alive. She was even up and about. Well, at least she was in the shade next to the hut, half upright and leaning against the wall.

Sofia felt a great joy filling her body. Could it be true? Could it be that Rosa was getting better, in spite of what Dr Nkeka had said? It might all have been a mistake. Maybe she had never caught that serious disease after all?

Rosa was alone at home.

She was lying outside the hut, but Lydia, Alfredo and Faustino were all away. Rosa looked at Sofia with her shiny eyes. Sofia realised that her joy would be short-lived. Rosa was as ill as she had been the night before.

'How do you feel?' Sofia asked cautiously.

'I can promise you one thing: you're feeling better than I do.'

The answer was like the vicious bite of an insect. Rosa had plunged her sting into Sofia. It was like the time when Rosa had thrown her crutches away. Sofia became sad.

'I just asked,' she said. 'That's all.'

'You already know the answer to that question,' Rosa hissed. She reached out to try to grab one of Sofia's crutches to make her fall over. Sofia saw it and managed to get out of the way.

'Where's Lydia?' Sofia asked, hoping to say something that would not irritate Rosa.

'Don't know.'

But Lydia never went anywhere without telling them where she was going.

Rosa wanted to be mean. Maybe she wanted to be left in peace. Sofia couldn't even find the energy to tell her what had happened that morning at Lydia's *machamba*.

She went inside and stretched out on the bed. She ought to eat something, but her appetite had gone. She looked around the room and thought of the morning's events. Then she thought of Rosa, who now hated her because she was well while Rosa was seriously ill.

Suddenly Sofia discovered that something about the room was different. At first she couldn't think what it was, and then she realised. The parcel with Cinnamonboy's clothes had disappeared. She remembered clearly that she had put it next to the sewing machine. Now it wasn't there.

She bent and looked under the bed but saw nothing there. She went into the other room and looked around. No parcel. She went out in the yard. Rosa was lying down, but she was still awake.

'Have you seen the parcel I put next to the sewing machine?' Sofia asked.

Rosa sat up slowly.

'What parcel?'

Sofia sensed that something was not right.

'There were clothes in it. Some clothes that I had mended.'

'Someone came to pick it up.'

'Who came?'

'Some boy. He wanted to pay, but I told him you'd promised to do it for free.'

Sofia felt cold. How could Rosa do this to her?

'Didn't he say what he was called?'

'Might have. I've forgotten. Anyway, I said that you had let me know that you didn't want to mend any more of his worn clothes.'

Sofia felt so furious she could have hit Rosa, but she managed to control herself.

Rosa leaned back again. Sofia couldn't think of anything to say. Rosa behaved as if she would have liked to infect Sofia with the illness she was carrying.

Rosa looked at Sofia.

'I just did as I thought right and proper,' she said, and smiled.

Sofia didn't answer. She went away, back into the hut and lay down on the bed. Cinnamonboy would never come back again. Rosa had chased him away.

Everything would have been all right if Sofia had not gone to the *machamba* instead of Lydia and stayed there all night. Now it was too late. Sofia didn't know his name or where he lived. He would never come back again.

If Rosa had been well, Sofia would have hated her for what she had done. Hating her now was impossible.

214

Sofia got out her diary and pencil. She wrote:

> *Now I have learnt that death takes more than a person's life. Sometimes death makes a good person bad. No, not bad. But fearful. And envious, too, jealous of the living. In spite of being so angry with Rosa, I must try to understand her. It's not easy. Perhaps impossible?*

She felt too tired to write any more. She put the diary back under her pillow, closed her eyes and fell asleep.

In her dream, the digger came crawling towards her. This time it really was an insect. Something like a cockroach or maybe a large fly. She tried to run away, but the insect crawled as fast as she could run. All the time, she heard Mr Bastardo's laughter.

When she woke up, Lydia was leaning over her. Her eyes glowed with anger, which was rare. She was really furious this time.

'What do you think you're doing?' she asked. 'What's this you're doing to Rosa?'

Sofia sat up.

'What am I meant to have done?'

'She tells me you're trying to hit her.'

Lydia was so angry that her body was shaking. She squeezed Sofia's shoulder hard enough to make it hurt.

'How dare you get at your sister who's ill!'

The blow came from the empty air, a powerful slap on the cheek that made Sofia fly backwards and hit her head on the wall. Lydia had never struck her before. Never ever.

'Now you go outside and ask your sister to forgive you,' Lydia ordered. Then she left the room.

Sofia's cheek was burning. She thought of the boy who had collected his clothes while she was standing in the road preventing Mr Bastardo's digger from getting at the cultivated fields.

Take me away from this place, Sofia thought. This is the end. I don't want to do any more for anyone. Rosa can die on her own. Lydia can fight for her plot together with the other women. I have no legs. I'm weary and too tired.

TWENTY-FOUR

∽

It was as if the words had been bleeding. The words were coming from Rosa's mouth. They were blackened, burnt to fragments. Words filled with shame and fear.

Sofia was standing in the yard. 'There's no way I can ask for forgiveness. I have done nothing,' she said.

Rosa burst into tears. Nothing she had said to Lydia was true. She didn't know why she had accused Sofia of having hit her.

Lydia was baffled. Now she was not shaking Sofia by her shoulder, but Rosa.

'Was all that untrue?'

'Yes it was.'

'Why do you say things that are not true?'

'I don't know.'

Sofia wanted Lydia to stop questioning Rosa.

She understood why Rosa had done this. When Sofia had been in hospital, she had wanted to do bad things, too.

Sofia went to the kitchen shed and drank some water. Lydia came after her.

'I shouldn't have hit you.'

Sofia looked straight into her mother's eyes when she answered.

'No,' she said. 'That's right. You shouldn't have hit me.'

Sofia could forgive Rosa, but not Lydia. Not yet anyway.

Then Sofia told Lydia what had happened. She described how the digger had come along, and Mr Bastardo. Lydia listened, first anxiously and then with growing amazement.

'Is this really true?' she asked when Sofia had fallen silent. 'You did that? Went to stand in the road. And the others followed you?'

'Ask them. Anyway, the important thing is that Mr Bastardo said he might be coming back. And bringing lots of policemen.'

'I'll go there tonight,' Lydia said. 'Please, can you forgive me for hitting you?'

'Not just now,' Sofia said. 'But maybe tomorrow.'

The evening came. Rosa sat with them by the fire but only picked at her supper. Lydia was nervous. She talked non-stop, about everything and nothing. This was what she often did when she was troubled.

Rosa went inside the hut to sleep. When she got up, she staggered and almost fell. She's becoming like her hoe, Sofia thought. First she dropped it. Now she's almost dropping herself.

Lydia got ready to go to the field and guard it.

'Do you think he'll really be back?' she asked. 'And bring the police?'

'I don't know,' Sofia replied.

Lydia disappeared into the dark night. In spite of Sofia's protests, she took Faustino with her. 'I'm sure the police won't beat up women with babies on their backs,' she said.

Sofia wasn't so sure, but Lydia was determined and left with Faustino tied to her back.

Alfredo came and sat down next to Sofia. She sensed that there was something he wanted to say. Alfredo often took his time before saying what he had been thinking about.

A woman was singing somewhere and Sofia thought her voice beautiful. The notes were rising and falling in the dark distance.

'Armando,' Alfredo said.

Sofia had been lost in thought and was not listening to him.

'What did you say?'

'Armando.'

'Who's that?'

'He.'

'He, who?'

'He who came to collect his clothes.'

Sofia stared at Alfredo. Was she really hearing this?

'Are you sure?'

'I was listening when he and Rosa were talking. She asked him what he was called. He said Armando.'

'Just Armando? Nothing else?'

'Saia.'

Sofia thought it an odd name. Maybe Alfredo had misheard.

'Armando Saia? Is that his name?'

'Yes.'

Alfredo seemed certain and quite proud of himself. Sofia believed that he had got it right. The boy was called Armando Saia.

Dreamy images started whirling around in Sofia's mind. Armando and Sofia. Sofia and Armando. Sofia Saia.

The images seemed to be dancing in the flames of the fire.

'Did he say where he lived?'

'No.'

'Which way did he walk off in when he left?'

'He didn't walk. He cycled.'

Sofia heard the longing in Alfredo's voice when he spoke about cycling. Alfredo's dream was a bicycle of his own. It was far too grand a dream to come true, of course. Neither Lydia nor Sofia could even imagine having enough money to spare for a bicycle for Alfredo.

'He went that way,' Alfredo said, and pointed.

The downhill stretch of the road. The direction he had taken when he vanished from the encounter with Sofia that moonlit night.

'Watch the fire for me,' Sofia said, and got up.

Alfredo became worried at once.

'Where are you going?'

'Only across to Mr Temba's. I'll be back soon.'

'I saw him go into *A Gorda's* place just now.'

Sofia thought that Alfredo's eyes could see through everything, the dark night, too. He did not only observe people, he gave them his own names. *A Gorda* was Mrs Mukulela. He called Mr Temba *O Chapeu*.

Sofia felt hesitant. Would she dare go and knock on Mrs Mukulela's door? What if she disturbed them at some awkward moment? Could they really have gone to bed already? It was still quite early in the evening.

The boy was so important to Sofia. Armando Saia. Mr Temba knew everybody in the nearby villages by name. If there were a Saia family somewhere, Mr Temba would be able to tell Sofia where to find it.

She walked off through the darkness towards Mrs Mukulela's place.

When she got there the door was closed. She was just about to knock when she heard sounds from inside. Mrs Mukulela's laugh. A kind of delighted growl from Mr Temba. Then complaining bed-springs from Mrs Mukulela's groaning bed.

A faint line of light showed in the crack between the door and the doorframe. Sofia could not resist the temptation. She peeped through the crack. There were a couple of lit candles on a small table. The light fell on Mrs Mukulela and Mr Temba, who were in bed together. Both were naked. Mr Temba was lying on top of Mrs Mukulela. She almost seemed to wrap her huge body round him.

Sofia backed away. Then she bent over to see more. She had never seen a man and a woman together like that before. They were both laughing. Sofia saw Mrs Mukulela's teeth gleam in the dark. Her hands were clasping Mr Temba's back. Sofia felt happy about what she was seeing. Two people could not get any closer than this. Then she started giggling at the thought that Mr Temba had actually taken his hat off.

Sofia went away. They deserved to be left in peace, even though she would have liked to watch them for longer.

When she got back home, Alfredo had fallen asleep by the fire. She shook him awake and he stumbled away to sleep inside. Sofia threw a few branches on the fire to make it flare up and she lay down beside it, staring into the flames.

Sofia was sleeping. Someone was shaking her awake. It was Mr Temba.

'I was just on my way home to get some sleep,' he said. 'I noticed that you were sleeping out here.'

Sofia felt confused. It was still dark. Had she been asleep for a long time?

Mr Temba seemed to guess what she was thinking.

'That awful rooster will start crowing soon,' he said.

By now Sofia was fully awake.

'I've met someone called Armando Saia,' she said. 'Mr Temba, do you know a Saia family?'

Mr Temba thought about it. He didn't ask her why she wanted to know.

'There is a family called Saia,' he said, after a while. 'They live very near the river, down there.' He pointed into the dark. 'Now, the man in the house is a car mechanic,' he went on. 'His name is Carlos. There's a son, and his name might be Armando.'

Then Mr Temba doffed his hat and disappeared in the night.

Sofia didn't feel sleepy any more. The embers of the fire were still glowing.

She was thinking about the boy. She knew more about him now. He tore holes in his trousers. He smelt of cinnamon. His surname was Saia. Also, he owned a bicycle and lived in a house by the river.

She also knew that Rosa had chased him away, but tried to ignore grim thoughts like that. She couldn't cope with them just now.

The rooster started to crow. Sofia stayed sitting by the fire. Her head felt empty.

Then dawn arrived. She rose, kicked sand over the embers and went inside. Maybe she could get another hour of sleep in her bed.

Then she heard a sharp, loud noise. A bang.

She listened. Another bang.

The sound came from far away. She thought that maybe something had fallen down. There was that loud, crackling noise again.

She knew then. It was gunfire.

The police, she thought.

Mr Bastardo has brought his policemen and now they're shooting at the women.

More bangs. Sofia hurried away, moving as fast as she could.

Nothing must happen to Lydia. Nothing.

TWENTY-FIVE

When Sofia arrived at the fields it was all over. The sun had risen over the horizon and it was morning. The road was full of people.

Sofia had been running along the last bit of the way, even though she actually could not run. All the time she had been thinking of the terrible things that might have happened. The women lying in the road, shot and dying. Lydia and Faustino, dead.

Lydia was alive. Faustino was alive, too.

There were policemen with rifles in their hands everywhere. First the digger had looked like a giant crawling insect, and now the grey-uniformed police were like an army of ants that had emerged from an anthill. They looked like termites.

Mr Bastardo had come along, but just as Sofia arrived, he was stepping into his black car to drive away.

No one had been shot.

The crowd in the road was milling about, seemingly out of control, and people were very upset. Sofia's relief when she discovered Lydia among the other women was indescribable.

Sofia pushed people aside to get to Lydia.

'I heard gunfire,' she said.

'There's been shooting, but not at us,' Lydia said. 'They shot straight up into the air. When we still didn't move they gave up. Mr Bastardo has been shouting his head off, saying he'll be back. He hasn't got a chance. The police won't shoot at us. Just into the air. Now they know for sure that we aren't scared of them.'

The women cheered as the digger and the policemen drove off. Mr Bastardo had already disappeared.

Now the women started dancing right there, in the middle of the road. Sofia was watching Lydia, following the way she moved her body to the beat of the rhythm. She danced very well. Faustino was awake. The movements of Lydia's body meant that he swung and leapt where he sat on her back.

Lydia and the other women stayed to work in their plots.

Sofia went home. She had to stop several times to adjust her leg-straps. It didn't matter. She could take it easy now.

Suddenly she felt as if Maria was walking beside her.

She was wearing her white dress and she walked close to Sofia.

'Tell me what's been happening,' Maria asked her.

Sofia told her. She explained about Mr Bastardo and his big digger, and the sour smell of gunpowder over the road to the fields.

Maria listened. Then she asked about Rosa. Sofia told her that Rosa was seriously ill. That she would die.

Maria didn't seem surprised. Sofia thought that she ought to ask Maria about so many things and especially what it was like after you had died. The trouble was that Maria seemed to disappear every time Sofia began formulating a question in her head.

Silently, Maria stayed at her side almost all the way back home. It was only when Sofia had come really close that she sensed Maria had left her.

Rosa was sitting with her back against the wall of the hut. Sofia thought that she was growing thinner and thinner. The skin was already tightly drawn round her legs.

Sofia stopped in the middle of the yard and looked around. Everything looked just the same as ever. But it was not the same. Rosa's illness meant that nothing was the same as before. Even the sand was different, although Sofia could not say why that should be.

She went into the hut, settled down on the edge of her bed and started writing in her diary.

Not about what had happened at the fields, not yet. It could wait. Something else occupied her mind. She wanted to set out a list of wishes. It would make clear to herself what it was she wanted most of all. It took her a long time to think out, but finally she decided how she wanted the list. She knew, of course, that many of her wishes would never come true. Still, nobody could stop her from wishing:

1. *Maria alive*
2. *Rosa well*
3. *Legs (my old, real ones)*
4. *Legs (my old, real ones)—better wish for that twice*
5. *The boy on the bicycle—Armando Saia*
6. *Children*
7. *Become a doctor*
8. *Soon be able to go to school again*
9. *Lydia to live for a thousand years*
10. *A good ink-pen*

Then she read through what she had written. She thought the list could have been much longer but these were the important wishes, and the order was right. She wished that Rosa would be well again, and that Maria had never died, more than anything else.

Evening came and Lydia returned from the fields.

She was in a good mood. It was almost as if, for a while at least, she had forgotten that Rosa was ill. Lydia could only have one big, strong feeling at a time, Sofia thought. Now she was full of her joy that they had driven Mr Bastardo off their land.

'They say he was going to use our fields to build something called a "golf course". Do you know what that means?'

Sofia had not heard the words before.

'The vegetables are growing well,' Lydia said. 'There's been just enough rain. I'll be able to start selling at the market by the beginning of next week.'

That's why she's so pleased, Sofia thought. It's not just because they've chased Mr Bastardo away. It's much more important that she'll soon be able to sell her vegetables. The money would go on corn and rice and oil.

Lydia went to bed early. Rosa was asleep already.

Sofia thought that sleep might be a way to get used to being dead. Then she cast the thought out of her head. She didn't want to think about it any more.

Maybe there was something that could be done after all to make Rosa wake up one morning and know that she was well again. Lydia had spoken of doctors other than Dr Nkeka, and *curandieros* other than Mr Nombora.

They mustn't give up. One mustn't weaken in a fight between life and death.

Sofia threw some more firewood on the fire.

First she was lying on her side, looking into the flames. Then she turned on to her back. She discovered that it was a full moon. She had forgotten about the moon.

The sky was cloudless, the moon distinct with its dark shadowy patches. She was breathing deeply and images were rushing round in her mind.

I'm an adult now, she thought.

My sister will die. Then I'll have two dead sisters. I must bear this. Think about those who are alive. She turned her head.

It seemed to her she had just travelled between the moon and the fire. Did any answers actually exist? Why should anyone be alive? Where did people come from? Where is death? Why did death exist? Why had death moved up close behind Rosa and chilled her with its breath?

More and more questions, but still no answers. She turned her head back towards the moon. A night-bird flapped past, its wings making a hissing noise in the air. Then she heard something new.

It was a rustling sound. Or maybe rattling. It came from the road. It might be made by bicycle tyres against gravel.

She sat up and looked along the road. She saw the faint light of a bicycle lamp.

It came closer and then it went out. The cyclist had stopped.

Could it be?

Sofia hardly dared to believe it. She rose and slowly walked to the road. She prepared herself for disappointment.

It was he. Moonboy, Cinnamonboy, Sergio, Zé, and finally, Armando.

All his names rushed through her head. She noticed that he was wearing the trousers she had mended.

'I just came by to thank you,' he said.

Sofia remembered Rosa's instructions. Not too interested, not too inviting.

'Just came by? In the middle of the night?'

He laughed.

'No, not really,' he said. 'But I like cycling about at night. In the dark.'

'Why do you?'

'I don't know.'

The short exchange stopped. What do I do now? Sofia asked herself. What's the right way to behave? He mustn't go away.

'The trousers turned out just fine,' Armando said.

'Rosa told me you had come for your clothes.'

'I don't think she liked me.' Suddenly his voice sounded a little sad.

Sofia felt that she had to defend Rosa.

'My sister is very ill.'

'I noticed that.'

'What did you notice?'

'That she's thin and pale.'

'I'm not ill.' The words jumped out of Sofia's mouth without warning. I'm such an idiot, she thought. Why did I say that?

Armando didn't seem to mind.

'Neither am I,' he said.

Their talk died away again.

Sofia thought that she must keep him there at any cost. If he went away now he might never come back again.

'It's a warm night,' she said.

'Yes it is.'

'The moon is full.'

'Yes.'

'I like you so very much.'

This time Sofia almost lost her grip on the crutches. The words were jumping out again.

She had said it! 'I like you so very much.'

'I like you, too,' Armando said. 'Not that we know each other. But anyway.'

'Anyway, what?'

'The bicycle seemed to want to take me back here.

I must've been disappointed when you weren't here yesterday.'

He wheeled his bicycle forward so that he could stand close to her. Sofia touched the handlebars. She dared not look up into his eyes. She could sense his cinnamon smell.

Then she looked up. He was looking at her.

'I must cycle back home now,' he said. 'But I'll come back to see you. If you like?'

'Yes, please, thank you.'

Now she was being silly again. Of course you mustn't say 'thank you'.

Armando cycled away.

Now she knew what happiness was like.

No need to ask the fire. The answer came from where it had to, from inside herself.

EPILOGUE

∾∾

Rosa died one afternoon, just after a thunderstorm had passed over and gone away. The beat of raindrops against the roof was becoming quieter. Rosa's life faded into silence the same way. It was like a slow wave, rocking to stillness against the beach and vanishing.

Rosa died in Sofia's bed. Lydia and Sofia were sitting by her, clasping her hands. Alfredo sat at the end of the bed, holding on to one of her feet.

Rosa was very thin when she died. Her face was covered in sores. She had been sleeping for most of the last months of her life. Now and then she woke up, as if to reassure herself that everybody was there as they should be. Then she would fall asleep again.

Once, when Sofia was alone with her, Rosa said something unforgettable.

'I'm not afraid any more. I'm not afraid now.'

Six months had passed since Lydia and the other women had forced Mr Bastardo to leave their land alone. During that time, Rosa had slowly become more and more ill. Dr Nkeka had visited a couple of times. He said that nothing could be done to save her.

Lydia understood well enough, but she still could not accept that Rosa must die.

Raindrops were dripping on the roof. Alfredo was holding Rosa's foot.

Then her life ended.

They buried her the following day. Mr Temba walked the whole long way to Boane and bought the coffin.

Lydia cried almost all the time. Sofia felt that she had to be the strong one. Mother for her own mother.

Rosa was buried among the other dead on a hill near the river. Sofia thought that she and Maria would meet each other now. At least Rosa would not have to be alone. Maria had been on her own for so long.

She also thought that when she had grown older, she must have two daughters, one called Maria and another called Rosa.

Armando did not come to the funeral. Sofia knew that he was somewhere nearby.

In the evening after Rosa's funeral, Sofia sat alone by the fire.

Lydia had been exhausted and gone to bed early. Sofia sat alone, looking into the fire for answers, but thinking now and then that she was being childish. The fire does not have a voice. There were no answers for her in the flames.

Suddenly, she started. There was a face on the other side of the fire. It seemed to her that the eyes and mouth and shining cheeks emerged from the flames.

She recognised that face.

It was Armando.

That night, the fire was scented by the wondrous spice called cinnamon.

ABOUT HIV AND AIDS

Sofia came to know a lot about the virus that made Rosa ill and finally killed her. Everyone should know about it, but of course it is possible to learn without having to observe someone who is close to you fall ill and die.

The virus is called HIV
HIV is short for Human Immunodeficiency Virus. The main effect of the virus is to slowly weaken the body's defences against many different illnesses. The body has many such defences, grouped together as the 'immune system'.

AIDS is the most common outcome of HIV infection
HIV-infected people are more likely to be attacked by special types of illnesses. These vary in different parts of the world.

When an infected person, anywhere, has become very weak and begins to fall ill from the typical diseases, that person is said to have AIDS, which is short for Acquired Immune Deficiency Syndrome. Because someone with AIDS is so weakened, the illnesses quickly become severe.

Getting better?
Rosa got hardly any medicine at all because she was a poor person living in a poor country. Rich people in rich countries have the best chance of helpful treatment and live for longer, but only get better for a while—not well. Medicines can help against some of the AIDS diseases for some time at least, but the only real cure must destroy all HIV in the infected person. This is not possible yet. It is incredibly

239

difficult to kill off the virus or prepare a good vaccine against it.

Catching HIV

Sofia is right to worry about getting infected while making love. Having sex with someone who is infected carries a very high risk of HIV infection. The important thing is not the sex act but contact with fluids made in the infected person's body.

Most of the HIV is in the blood. That is why HIV on syringe needles or in blood transfusions is just as dangerous as sex with an infected person. It is also why new-born babies can get infected by their mother's blood and even by breast milk (HIV from the mother's blood can get into the milk). Anyone caring for someone like Rosa, with open wounds, runs some risk of infection from contact with infected blood.

Some body fluids contain less HIV than others. Saliva has hardly any, which is important to know, too. It means that being near an infected person, who talks or coughs or sneezes, and so on, is not at all dangerous. Mouth-to-mouth resuscitation is not dangerous either.

Don't catch HIV in the first place

Sofia is right about how important it is to use condoms. Using a condom is an easy way of preventing people's body fluids from mixing while they are having sex. Other ways of being careful are all based on the same idea, which is to avoid contact with the infected person's body fluids and especially blood.